FIVE RUN AWAY TOGETHER

The third story of the Famous Five

The FAMOUS FIVE *are*
Julian, Dick, George (Georgina by rights),
Anne, and Timothy the dog

The Five are together again at Kirrin
Cottage. Because George's mother is ill, they
are left in the very unsatisfactory care of Mrs.
Stick, who has an unpleasant son, and a
sailor husband. To get away from the Sticks,
they hide on Kirrin Island

But they do not so easily escape. The Sticks,
too, appear on the island. Their nefarious
activities, and signals from a boat at sea,
make the children suspect smuggling, but a
child's scream alters the whole picture

And Timothy lives up to his reputation

Enid Blyton

Five run
away together

Illustrated by Eileen Soper

KNIGHT BOOKS
the paperback division of Brockhampton Press

ISBN 0 340 02462 3

This edition first published 1967 by Knight Books,
the paperback division of Brockhampton Press Ltd.
Leicester
Eighth impression 1973

Printed and bound in Great Britain by
Cox & Wyman Ltd, London, Reading and Fakenham

First published by Hodder & Stoughton Ltd. 1944
Thirteenth impression 1964
Reissued by Brockhampton Press Ltd.

CONTENTS

1	Summer holidays	7
2	The Stick family	16
3	A nasty shock	24
4	A few little upsets	33
5	In the middle of the night	41
6	Julian defeats the Sticks	49
7	Better news	58
8	George's plan	65
9	An exciting night	73
10	Kirrin Island once more	83
11	On the old wreck	91
12	The cave in the cliff	98
13	A day on the Island	105
14	Disturbance in the night	113
15	Who is on the island?	123
16	The Sticks get a fright	130
17	A shock for Edgar	139
18	An unexpected prisoner	147
19	A scream in the night	156
20	A rescue – and a new prisoner!	163
21	A visit to the police station	172
22	Back to Kirrin Island!	181

Chapter One

SUMMER HOLIDAYS

'GEORGE dear, do settle down and do something,' said George's mother. 'You keep wandering in and out with Timothy, and I am trying to have a rest.'

'Sorry, Mother,' said Georgina, taking hold of Timothy's collar. 'But I feel lonely without the others. Oh I do wish tomorrow would come. I've been without them for three whole weeks already.'

Georgina went to boarding-school with her cousin Anne, and in the holidays she and Anne, and Anne's two brothers, Julia and Dick, usually joined up together and had plenty of fun. Now it was the summer holidays, and already three weeks had gone by. Anne, Dick and Julian had gone away with their father and mother, but Georgina's parents had wanted their little girl with them, so she had not gone.

Now her three cousins were coming the next day to spend the rest of the summer holidays with her at her old home, Kirrin Cottage.

'It will be lovely when they are here,' said George, as she was always called, to Timothy her dog. 'Simply lovely, Timothy. Don't you think so?'

'Woof,' said Timothy and licked George's bare knee.

George was dressed, as usual, exactly like a boy, in shorts and jersey. She had always wanted to be a boy, and would never answer if she was called Georgina. So everyone called her George. She had missed her cousins very much during the first weeks of the summer holidays.

'I used to think I liked best to be alone,' George said to Timothy, who always seemed to understand every word she said. 'But now I know that was silly. It's nice to be with others and share things, and make friends.'

Timothy thumped his tail on the ground. He certainly liked being with the other children too. He was longing to see Julian, Anne and Dick again.

George took Timothy down to the beach. She shaded her eyes with her hand, and looked out to the entrance of the bay. In the middle of it, almost as if it were guarding it, lay a small, rocky island, on which rose the ruins of an old castle.

'We'll visit you again this summer, Kirrin Island,' said George softly. 'I haven't been able to go to you yet this summer, because my boat was being mended – but it will be ready soon, then I'll come to you. And I'll look all round the old castle again. Oh Tim – do you remember the adventures we had on Kirrin Island last summer?'

Tim remembered quite well, because he himself had shared in the thrilling adventures. He had been down in the dungeons of the castle with the others; he had helped to find treasure there, and had had just as grand a time as the four children he loved. He gave a little bark.

'You're remembering, aren't you, Tim?' said George, patting him. 'Won't it be fun to go there again? We'll go down into the dungeons again, shall we? And oh! – do you remember how Dick climbed down the deep well-shaft to rescue us?'

It was exciting, remembering all the things that had

happened last year. It made George long all the more for the next day, when her three friends would arrive.

'I wish Mother would let us go and live on the island for a week,' thought George. 'That would be the greatest fun we could have. To live on my very own island!'

It *was* George's island. It really belonged to her mother, but she had said, two or three years back, that George could have it, and George now thought of it as really her own. She felt that all the rabbits on it belonged to her, all the wild birds and other creatures.

'I'll suggest that we go there for a week, when the

others come,' she thought, excitedly. 'We'll take our food
and everything, and live there quite by ourselves. We
shall feel like Robinson Crusoe.'

She went to meet her cousins the next day, driving the
pony and trap by herself. Her mother wanted to come,
but she said she did not feel very well. George felt a bit
worried about her. So often lately her mother had said
she didn't feel very well. Perhaps it was the heat of the
summer. The weather had been so very hot lately. Day
after day had brought nothing but blue sky and sunshine.
George had been burnt a dark-brown, and her eyes were
startlingly blue in her sunburnt face. She had had her
hair cut even shorter than usual, and it really was difficult to know whether she was a boy or a girl.

The train came in. Three hands waved madly from a
window, and George shouted in delight.

'Julian! Dick! Anne! You're here at last.'

The three children tumbled pell-mell out of their car-
riage. Julian yelled to a porter.

'Our bags are in the guard's van. Hallo, George! How
are you? Golly, you've grown.'

They all had. They were all a year older and a year
bigger than when they had had their exciting adventures
on Kirrin Island. Even Anne, the youngest, didn't look
such a small girl now. She flung herself on George, almost
knocking her over, and then went down on her knees beside Timothy, who was quite mad with joy to see his three
friends.

There was a terrific noise. They all shouted their news
at once, and Timothy barked without stopping.

'We thought the train would never get here!'

'Oh Timothy, you darling, you're just the same as ever!'

'Woof, woof, woof!'

'Mother's sorry she couldn't come and meet you too.'

'George, how brown you are! I say aren't we going to have fun.'

'Woof, Woof!'

'Shut up, Tim darling, and do get down; you've bitten my tie almost in half. Oh, you dear old dog, it's grand to see you!'

'Woof!'

The porter wheeled up their luggage, and soon it was in the pony-cart. George clicked to the waiting pony, and it cantered off. The five in the little cart all talked at once at the top of their voices, Tim far more loudly than anyone else, for his doggy voice was strong and powerful.

'I hope your mother isn't ill?' said Julian, who was fond of his Aunt Fanny. She was gentle and kind, and loved having them all.

'I think it must be the heat,' said George.

'What about Uncle Quentin?' asked Anne. 'Is he all right?'

The three children did not very much like George's father, because he could get into very fierce tempers, and although he welcomed the three cousins to his house, he did not really care for children. So they always felt a little awkward with him, and were glad when he was not there.

'Father's all right,' said George, cheerfully. 'Only he's worried about Mother. He doesn't seem to notice her much when she's well and cheerful, but he gets awfully upset if anything goes wrong with her. So be a bit careful

of him at the moment. You know what he's like when he's
worried.'

The children did know. Uncle Quentin was best
avoided when things went wrong. But not even the
thought of a cross uncle could damp them today. They
were on holiday; they were going to Kirrin Cottage; they
were by the sea, and there was dear old Timothy beside
them, and fun of all kinds in store for them.

'Shall we go to Kirrin Island, George?' asked Anne.
'Do let's! We haven't been there since last summer. The
weather was too bad in the winter and Easter holidays.
Now it's gorgeous.'

'Of course we'll go,' said George, her blue eyes shining. 'Do you know what I thought? I thought it would
be marvellous to go and stay there for a whole week by
ourselves! We are older now, and I'm sure Mother would
let us.'

'Go and stay on your island for a week!' cried Anne.
'Oh! That would be too good to be true.'

'*Our* island,' said George, happily. 'Don't you remember I said I would divide it into four, and we'd all share
it? Well, I meant it, you know. It's ours, not mine.'

'What about Timothy?' said Anne. 'Oughtn't he to
have a share as well? Can't we make it five bits, one for
him too?'

'He can share mine,' said George. She drew the pony
to a stop, and the four children and the dog gazed out
across the blue bay. 'There's Kirrin Island,' said George.
'Dear little island. I can hardly wait to get to it now. I
haven't been able to go there yet, because my boat wasn't
mended.'

'Then we can all go together,' said Dick. 'I wonder if the rabbits are just as tame as ever.'

'Woof!' said Timothy at once. He had only to hear the word 'rabbits' to get excited.

'It's no good your thinking about the rabbits on Kirrin,' said George. 'You know I don't allow you to chase them, Tim.'

Timothy's tail dropped and he looked mournfully at George. It was the only thing on which he and George did not agree. Tim was firmly convinced that rabbits were meant for him to chase, and George was just as firmly convinced that they were not.

'Get on!' said George to the pony, and jerked the reins. The little creature trotted on towards Kirrin Cottage, and very soon they were all opposite the front gate.

A sour-faced woman came out from the back door to help them down with their luggage. The children did not know her.

'Who's she?' they whispered to George.

'The new cook,' said George. 'Joanna had to go and look after her mother, who broke her leg. Then Mother got this cook – Mrs. Stick her name is.'

'Good name for her,' grinned Julian. 'She looks a real old stick! But all the same I hope she doesn't stick here for long. I hope Joanna comes back. I liked old fat Joanna, and she was nice to Timmy.'

'Mrs. Stick has a dog too,' said George. 'A dreadful animal, smaller than Tim, all sort of mangy and moth-eaten. Tim can't bear it.'

'Where is it?' asked Anne, looking round.

'It's kept in the kitchen, and Tim isn't allowed near

it,' said George. 'Good thing too, because I'm sure he'd eat it! He can't think what's in the kitchen, and goes sniffing round the shut door till Mrs. Stick nearly goes mad.'

The others laughed. They had all climbed down from the pony-cart now, and were ready to go indoors. Julian had helped Mrs. Stick in with all the bags. George took the pony-cart away, and the other three went in to say how-do-you-do to their uncle and aunt.

'Well, dears,' said Aunt Fanny, smiling at them from the sofa where she was lying down. 'How are you all? I'm sorry I could not come to meet you. Uncle Quentin is out for a walk. You had better go upstairs, and wash and change. Then come down for tea.'

The boys went up to their old bedroom, with its queer slanting roof, and its window looking out over the bay. Anne went to the little room she shared with George. How good it was to be back again at Kirrin! What fun they would have these holidays with George and dear old Timmy!

Chapter Two

THE STICK FAMILY

IT was lovely to wake up the next morning at Kirrin Cottage and see the sun shining in at the windows, and to hear the far-off plash-plash-plash of the sea. It was gorgeous to leap out of bed and rush to see how blue the sea was, and how lovely Kirrin Island looked at the entrance of the bay.

'I'm going for a bathe before breakfast,' said Julian, and snatched up his bathing-drawers. 'Coming, Dick?'

'You bet!' said Dick. 'Call the girls. We'll all go.'

So down they went, the four of them, with Tim galloping behind them, his tail wagging nineteen to the dozen, and his long pink tongue hanging out of his mouth. He went into the water with the others, and swam all round them. They were all good swimmers, but Julian and George were the best.

They put towels round themselves, rubbed their bodies dry and pulled on shorts and jerseys. Then back to breakfast they went, as hungry as hunters. Anne noticed a boy in the back garden and stared in surprise.

'Who's that?' she said

'Oh, that's Edgar, Mrs. Stick's boy,' said George. 'I don't like him. He does silly things, like putting out his tongue and calling rude names.'

Edgar appeared to be singing when the others went in at the gate. Anne stopped to listen.

'Georgie-Porgie, pudding and pie!' sang Edgar, a silly look on his face. He seemed about thirteen or fourteen, a stupid, yet sly-looking youth. 'Georgie-porgie pudding and pie!'

George went red. 'He's always singing that,' she said, furiously. 'Just because I'm called "George," I suppose. He thinks he's clever. I can't bear him.'

Julian called out to Edgar. 'You shut up! You're not funny, only jolly silly!'

'Georgie-porgie,' began Edgar again, a silly smile on his wide red face. Julian made a step towards him, and he at once disappeared into the house.

'Shan't stand much of *him*,' said Julian, in a decided voice. 'I wonder *you* do, George. I wonder you haven't slapped his face, stamped on his foot, bitten his ears off and done a few other things! You used to be so fierce.'

'Well – I am still, really,' said George. 'I *feel* frightfully fierce down inside me when I hear Edgar singing silly songs at me like that and calling out names – but you see, Mother really hasn't been well, and I know jolly well if I go for Edgar, Mrs. Stick will leave, and poor old Mother would have to do all the work, and she really isn't fit to at present. So I just hold myself in, and hope that Timmy will do the same.'

'Good for *you*, old thing!' said Julian, admiringly, for he knew how hard it was for George to keep her temper at times.

'I think I'll just go up to Mother's room and see if she'd like breakfast in bed,' said George.

'Hang on to old Timmy a moment, will you? If Edgar appears again, he might go for him.'

Julian hung on to Timmy's collar. Timmy had growled when Edgar had been in the garden, now he stood stock still, his nose twitching as if he were trying to trace some smell.

Suddenly a mangy-looking dog appeared out of the kitchen door. It had a dirty white coat, out of which patches seemed to have been bitten, and its tail was well between its legs.

'Wooooof!' said Timmy, joyfully, and leapt at the dog. He pulled Julian over, for he was a big dog, and the boy let go his hold of the dog's collar. Timmy pounced excitedly on the other dog, who gave a fearful whine and tried to go into the kitchen door again.

'Timmy! Come here, sir!' yelled Julian. But Timmy didn't hear. He was busy trying to snap off the other dog's ears — or at least, that is what he appeared to be doing. The other dog yelled for help, and Mrs. Stick appeared at the kitchen door, a saucepan in her hand.

'Call off that dog!' she screeched. She hit out at Timmy with the saucepan, but he dodged and it hit her own dog instead, making it yelp all the more.

'Don't hit out with that!' said Julian. 'You'll hurt the dogs. Hi, Timmy, TIMMY!'

Edgar now appeared, looking very scared. He picked up a stone and seemed to be watching his chance to hurl it at Timmy. Anne shrieked.

'You're not to throw that stone; you're not to! You bad wicked boy!'

In the middle of all this turmoil Uncle Quentin appeared, looking angry and irritable.

'Good heavens! What is all this going on? I never heard such a row in my life.'

Then George appeared, flying out of the door like the wind, to rescue her beloved Timothy. She rushed to the two dogs and tried to pull Timmy away. Her father yelled at her.

'Come away, you little idiot! Don't you know better than to separate two fighting dogs with your bare hands? Where's the garden hose?'

It was fixed to a tap nearby. Julian ran to it and turned on the tap. He picked up the hose and turned it on the two dogs. At once the jet of water spurted out at them, and they leapt apart in surprise. Julian saw Edgar standing near, and couldn't resist swinging the hose a little so that the boy was soaked. He gave a scream and ran in at once.

'What did you do that for?' said Uncle Quentin, annoyed. 'George, tie Timothy up at once. Mrs. Stick didn't I tell you not to let your dog out of the kitchen unless you had him on a lead? I won't have this kind of thing happening. Where's the breakfast? Late as usual!'

Mrs. Stick disappeared into the kitchen, muttering and grumbling, taking her drenched dog with her. George, looking sulky, tied Timothy up. He lay down in his kennel, looking beseechingly at his mistress.

'I've told you not to take any notice of that mangy-looking dog,' said George, severely. 'Now you see what happens! You put Father into a bad temper for the rest of the day, and Mrs. Stick will be so angry she won't make any cakes for tea!'

Timmy gave a whine, and put his head down on his paws. He licked a few hairs from the corner of his mouth. It was sad to be tied up – but anyhow he had bitten a bit off the tip of one of that dreadful dog's ears!

They all went in to breakfast. 'Sorry I let Timmy go,' said Julian to George. 'But he nearly tore my arm off. I couldn't possibly hold him! He's grown into an awfully powerful dog, hasn't he?'

'Yes,' said George, proudly. 'He has. He could eat Mrs. Stick's dog up in a mouthful if we'd let him. And Edgar too.'

'And Mrs. Stick,' said Anne. 'All of them. I don't like any of them.'

Breakfast was rather a subdued meal, as Aunt Fanny was not there, but Uncle Quentin was – and Uncle Quentin in a bad temper was not a very cheerful person to have at the breakfast-table. He snapped at George and glared at the others. Anne almost wished they hadn't come to Kirrin Cottage! But her spirits rose when she thought of the rest of the day – they would take their dinner out, perhaps, and have it on the beach – or maybe even go out to Kirrin Island. Uncle Quentin wouldn't be with them to spoil things.

Mrs. Stick appeared to take away the porridge plates and bring in the bacon. She banged the plates down on the table.

'No need to do that,' said Uncle Quentin, irritably. Mrs. Stick said nothing. She was scared of Uncle Quentin, and no wonder! She put the next lot of plates down quietly.

'What are you going to do today?' asked Uncle

Quentin, towards the end of breakfast. He was feeling a little better by that time, and didn't like to see such subdued faces round him.

'We thought we might go out for a picnic,' said George, eagerly. 'I asked Mother. She said we might, if Mrs. Stick will make us sandwiches.'

'Well, I shouldn't think she'll try very hard,' said Uncle Quentin, trying to make a little joke. They all smiled politely. 'But you can ask her.'

There was a silence. Nobody liked the idea of asking Mrs. Stick for sandwiches.

'I do wish she hadn't brought Stinker,' said George, gloomily. 'Everything would be easier if he wasn't here.'

'Is that the name of her son?' asked Uncle Quentin, startled.

George grinned. 'Oh no. Though it wouldn't be a bad name for him, because he hardly ever has a bath, and he's jolly smelly. It's her dog I mean. She calls him Tinker, but I call him Stinker, because he really does smell awful.'

'I don't think it's a very nice name,' said her father, in the midst of the others' giggles.

'No, it isn't,' said George; 'but then, he isn't a very nice dog.'

In the end it was Aunt Fanny who saw Mrs. Stick and arranged about the sandwiches. Mrs. Stick went up to see Aunt Fanny, who was having breakfast in bed, and agreed to make sandwiches, though with a very bad grace.

'I didn't bargain for three more children to come traipsing along,' she said, sulkily.

'I told you they were coming, Mrs. Stick,' said Aunt Fanny, patiently. 'I didn't know I should be feeling so ill myself when they came. If I had been well I could have made their sandwiches and done many more things. I can only ask you to help as much as you can till I feel better. I may be all right tomorrow. Let the children have a good time for a week or so, and then, if I still feel ill, I am sure they will all turn to and help a bit. But let them have a good time first.'

The children took their packets of sandwiches and set off. On the way they met Edgar, looking as stupid and sly as usual. 'Why don't you let me come along with you?' he said. 'Let's go to that island. I know a lot about it, I do.'

'No, you don't,' said George, in a flash. 'You don't know anything about it. And I'd never take *you*. It's *my* island, see? Well, *ours*. It belongs to all four of us and Timmy, too. We should never allow you to go.'

' 'Tisn't your island,' said Edgar. 'That's a lie, that is!'

'You don't know what you're talking about,' said George, scornfully. 'Come on, you others! We can't waste time talking to Edgar.'

They left him, looking sulky and angry. As soon as they were at a safe distance he lifted up his voice:

> *'Georgie-porgie, pudding and pie,*
> *She knows how to tell a lie,*
> *Georgie-porgie, pudding and pie!'*

Julian made as if he would go back after the rude Edgar, but George pulled him on. 'He'll only go and tell tales to his mother, and she'll walk out and there'll be no one to help Mother,' she said. 'I'll just have to put up with it. We'll try and think of some way to get our own back, though. Nasty creature! I hate his pimply nose and screwed-up eyes.'

'Woof!' said Timmy, feelingly.

'Timmy says he hates Stinker's miserable tail and silly little ears,' explained George, and they all laughed. That made them feel better. They were soon out of hearing of Edgar's silly song, and forgot all about him.

'Let's go and see if your boat is ready,' said Julian. 'Then maybe we could row out to the dear old island.'

Chapter Three

A NASTY SHOCK

GEORGE'S boat was almost ready, but not quite. It was having a last coat of paint on it. It looked very gay, for George had chosen a bright red paint, and the oars were painted red too.

'Oh, can't we possibly have it this afternoon?' said George to Jim the boatman.

He shook his head.

'No, Master George,' he said, 'not unless you all want to be messed up with red paint. It'll be dry tomorrow, but not before.'

It always made the others smile to hear the boatmen and fishermen call Georgina 'Master George.' The local people all knew how badly she wanted to be a boy, and they knew, too, how plucky and straightforward she was, so they laughed to one another and said: 'Well, they reckoned she behaved like a boy, and if she wanted to be called "Master George" instead of "Miss Georgina", she deserved it!'

So Georgina was Master George, and enjoyed strutting about in her shorts and jersey on the beach, using her boat as well as any fisher-boy, and swimming faster than them all.

'We'll go to the island tomorrow then,' said Julian. 'We'll just picnic on the beach today. Then we'll go for a walk.'

So they picnicked on the sands with Timothy sharing more than half their lunch. The sandwiches were not very

nice. The bread was too stale; there was not enough butter inside, and they were far too thick. But Timothy
didn't mind. He gobbled up as many as he could, his tail
wagging so hard that it sent sand over everyone.

'Timothy, do take your tail out of the sand if you want
to wag it,' said Julian, getting sand all over his hair for
the fourth time. Timmy wagged his tail hard again, and
sent another shower over him. Everyone laughed.

'Let's go for a walk now,' said Dick, jumping up. 'My
legs could do with some good exercise. Where shall we
go?'

'We'll walk along the cliff-top, where we can see the island all the time, shall we?' said Anne. 'George, is the old wreck still there?'

George nodded. The children had once had a most exciting time with an old wreck that had lain at the bottom of the sea. A great storm had lifted it up and set it firmly on the rocks. They had been able to explore the wreck then, and had found a map of the castle in it, with instructions as to where hidden treasure was to be found.

'Do you remember how we found that old map in the wreck, and how we looked for the ingots of gold and found them?' said Julian, his eyes gleaming as he remembered it all. 'Isn't the wreck battered to pieces yet, George?'

'No,' said George. 'I don't think so. It's on the rocks on the other side of the island, you remember, so we can't see it from here. But we might have a look at it when we go on the island tomorrow.'

'Yes, let's,' said Anne. 'Poor old wreck! I guess it won't last many winters now.'

They walked along the cliff-top with Timothy capering ahead of them. They could see the island easily and the ruined castle rising up from the middle.

'There's the jackdaw tower,' said Anne, looking. 'The other tower's fallen down hasn't it? Look at the jackdaws circling round and round the tower, George!'

'Yes. They build in it every year,' said George. 'Don't you remember the masses of sticks round about the tower that the jackdaws dropped when they built their nests? We picked some up and made a fire with them once.'

'I'd like to do that again,' said Anne. 'I would really. Let's do it each night if we stay a week on the island. George, did you ask your mother?'

'Oh yes,' said George. 'She said she thought we might, but she would see.'

'I don't like it when grown-ups say they'll see,' said Anne. 'It so often means they won't let you do something after all, but they don't like to tell you at the time.'

'Well, I expect she will let us,' said George. 'After all, we're much older than last year. Why, Julian is in his teens already, and I soon shall be and so will Dick. Only Anne is small.'

'I'm not,' said Anne, indignantly. 'I'm as strong as you are. I can't help being younger.'

'Hush, hush, baby!' said Julian, patting his little sister on the back and laughing at her furious face. 'Hallo – look! What's that over there on the island?'

He had caught sight of something as he was teasing Anne. Everyone swung round and gazed at Kirrin. George gave an exclamation.

'Golly – a spire of smoke! Surely it's smoke! Someone's on my island.'

'On *our* island,' corrected Dick. 'It can't be! That smoke must come from a steamer out beyond the island. We can't see it, that's all. But I bet the smoke comes from a steamer. We know no one can get to the island but us. They don't know the way.'

'If anyone's on my island,' began George, looking very fierce and angry, 'if anyone's on my island, I'll – I'll – I'll...'

'You'll explode and go up in smoke!' said Dick.

'There – it's gone now. I'm sure it was only a steamer letting off steam or smoking hard, whatever they do.'

They watched Kirrin Island for some time after that, but they could see no more smoke. 'If only my boat was ready!' said George, restlessly. 'I'd go over this afternoon. I've a good mind to go and get my boat, even if the paint *is* wet.'

'Don't be an idiot!' said Julian. 'You know what an awful row we'd get into if we go home with all our things bright red. Have a bit of sense, George.'

George gave up the idea. She watched for a steamer to appear at one side of the island or another, to come into the bay, but none came.

'Probably anchored out there,' said Dick. 'Come on! Are we going to stand rooted to this spot for the rest of the day?'

'We'd better get back home,' said Julian, looking at his wrist-watch. 'It's almost tea-time. I hope your mother is up, George. It's much nicer when she's at meals.'

'Oh, I expect she will be,' said George. 'Come on, then let's go back!'

They turned to go back. They watched Kirrin Island as they walked, but all they could see was jackdaws or gulls in the sky above it. No more spires of smoke appeared. It must have been a steamer!

'All the same, I'm going over tomorrow to have a look,' said George, firmly. 'If any trippers are visiting my island I'll turn them off.'

'*Our* island,' said Dick. 'George, I wish you'd remember you said you'd share it with us.'

'Well – I did share it out with you,' said George, 'but

I can't help feeling it's still my island. Come on! I'm getting hungry.'

They came back at last to Kirrin Cottage. They went into the hall, and then into the sitting-room. To their great surprise Edgar was there, reading one of Julian's books.

'What are you doing here?' said Julian. 'And who told you you could borrow my book?'

'I'm not doing any harm,' said Edgar. 'If I want to have a quiet read, why shouldn't I?'

'You wait till my Father comes in and finds you lolling about here,' said George. 'My goodness, if you'd gone into his study, you'd have been sorry.'

'I've been in there,' said Edgar, surprisingly. 'I've seen those funny instruments he's working with.'

'How *dare* you!' said George, going white with rage. 'Why, even *we* are not allowed to go into my Father's study. As for touching his things – well!'

Julian eyed Edgar curiously. He could not imagine why the boy should suddenly be so insolent.

'Where's your father, George?' he said. 'I think it would be best to get him to deal with Edgar. He must be mad.'

'Call him if you like,' said Edgar, still lolling on the sofa, and flicking over the pages of Julian's book in a most irritating way. 'He won't come.'

'What do you mean?' said George, feeling suddenly scared. 'Where's my mother?'

'Call her too, if you like,' said the boy, looking sly. 'Go on! Call her.'

The children suddenly felt afraid. What did Edgar

mean? George flew upstairs to her mother's room, shouting loudly.

'Mother! Mother! Where are you?'

But her mother's bed was empty. It had not been
made – but it was empty. George flew into all the other
bedrooms, shouting desperately: 'Mother! Mother!
Father! Where are you?'

But there was no answer. George ran downstairs, her
face very white. Edgar grinned up at her.

'What did I tell you?' he said. 'I said you could call all
you liked, but they wouldn't come.'

'Where are they?' demanded George. 'Tell me at once!'

'Find out yourself,' said Edgar.

There was a resounding slap, and Edgar leapt to his
feet, holding his left cheek with his hand. George had
flown at him and dealt him the hardest smack she could.
Edgar lifted his hand to slap her back, but Julian stood
in front.

'You're not fighting George,' he said. 'She's a girl. If
you want a fight, I'll take you on.'

'I won't be a girl; I'm a boy!' shouted George, trying
to push Julian away. 'I'll fight Edgar, and I'll beat him,
you see if I don't.'

But Julian kept her off. Edgar began to edge towards
the doorway, but he found Dick there.

'One minute,' said Dick. 'Before you go – where are
our uncle and aunt?'

'Gr-r-r-r-r-r,' suddenly said Timothy, in such a
threatening voice that Edgar stared at him in fright. The
dog had bared his great teeth, and had put up the hackles
on his neck. He looked very frightening.

'Hold that dog!' said Edgar, his voice trembling. 'He looks as if he's going to spring at me.'

Julian put his hand on Tim's collar. 'Quiet, Tim!' he said. 'Now, Edgar, tell us what we want to know, and tell us quickly, or you'll be sorry.'

'Well, there isn't much to tell,' said Edgar, keeping his eye on Timothy. He shot a look at George and went on. 'Your mother was suddenly taken very ill – with a terrible pain *here* – and they got the doctor and they've taken her away to hospital, and your father went with her. That's all!'

George sat down on the sofa, looking paler still and rather sick.

'Oh!' she said. 'Poor Mother! I wish I hadn't gone out today. Oh dear – how can we find out what's happened?'

Edgar had slipped out of the room, shutting the door behind him so that Timmy should not follow. The kitchen door was slammed, too. The children stared at one another, feeling sorry and dismayed. Poor George! Poor Aunt Fanny!

'There must be a note somewhere,' said Julian, and looked round the room. He saw a letter stuck into the rim of the big mirror there, addressed to George. He gave it to her. It was from George's father.

'Read it, quickly,' said Anne. 'Oh dear – this is really a horrid beginning to our holidays here!'

Chapter Four

A FEW LITTLE UPSETS

GEORGE read the letter out loud. It was not very long, and had evidently been written in a great hurry.

DEAR GEORGE,

Your mother has been taken very ill. I am going with her to the hospital. I shall not leave her till she is getting better. That may be in a few days' time, or in a week's time. I will telephone to you each day at nine o'clock in the morning to tell you how she is. Mrs. Stick will look after you all. Try to manage all right till I come back.

Your loving
FATHER

'Oh dear!' said Anne, knowing how dreadful George must feel. George loved her mother dearly, and for once in a way the girl had tears in her eyes. George never cried – but it was terrible to come home and find her mother gone like this. And Father too! No one there but Mrs. Stick and Edgar.

'I can't bear Mother going like this,' sobbed George, suddenly, and buried her head in a cushion. 'She – she might never come back.'

'Don't be silly, George,' said Julian, sitting down and putting his arm round her. 'Of course she will. Why shouldn't she? Didn't your father say he was staying with her till she was getting better — and that would be probably in a few days' time. Cheer up, George! It isn't like you to give way like this.'

'But I didn't say good-bye,' sobbed poor George. 'And I made her ask Mrs. Stick for the sandwiches, instead of me. I want to go and find Mother and see how she is myself.'

'You don't know where they've taken her, and if you did, they wouldn't let you in,' said Dick, gently. 'Let's have some tea. We shall all feel better after that.'

'I couldn't eat *any*-thing,' said George, fiercely. Timothy pushed his nose into her hands, and tried to lick them. They were under her buried face. The dog whined a little.

'Poor Timmy! He can't understand,' said Anne. 'He's awfully upset because you are unhappy, George.'

That made George sit up. She rubbed her hands over her eyes, and let Timmy lick the wet tears off them. He looked surprised at the salty taste. He tried to get on to George's knee.

'Silly Timmy!' said George, in a more ordinary voice. 'Don't be upset. I just got a shock, that's all! I'm better now, Timmy. Don't whine like that, silly! I'm all right. I'm not hurt.'

But Timothy felt certain George was really hurt or injured in some way to cry like that, and he kept whining, and pawing at George, and trying to get on to her knee.

Julian opened the door. 'I'm going to tell Mrs. Stick we want our tea,' he said, and went out. The others thought he was rather brave to face Mrs. Stick.

Julian went to the kitchen door and opened it. Edgar was sitting there, one side of his face scarlet, where George had slapped it. Mrs. Stick was there, looking grim.

'If that girl slaps my Edgar again I'll be after her,' she said, threateningly.

'Edgar deserved what he got,' said Julian. 'Can we have some tea, please?'

'I've a good mind to get you none,' said Mrs. Stick. Her dog started up from its corner and growled at Julian. 'That's right, Tinker! You growl at folks that slap Edgar,' said Mrs. Stick.

Julian was not in the least afraid of Tinker. 'If you are not going to get us any tea, I'll get it myself,' said the boy. 'Where is the bread, and where are the cakes?'

Mrs. Stick stared at Julian, and the boy looked back at her steadfastly. He thought she was a most unpleasant woman, and he certainly was not going to allow her to get the better of him. He wished he could tell her to go – but he had a feeling that she wouldn't, so it would be a waste of his breath.

Mrs. Stick dropped her eyes first. 'I'll get your tea,' she said, 'but if I've any nonsense from you I'll get you no other meals.'

'And if I have any nonsense from you I shall go to the police,' said Julian, unexpectedly. He hadn't meant to say that. It came out quite suddenly, but it had a surprising effect on Mrs. Stick. She looked startled and alarmed.

'Now, there's no call to be nasty,' she said in a much more polite voice. 'We've all had a bit of a shock, and we're upset, like – I'll get you your tea right now.'

Julian went out. He wondered why his sudden threat of going to the police had made Mrs. Stick so much more polite. Perhaps she was afraid the police would get on to his Uncle Quentin and he would come tearing back. Uncle Quentin wouldn't care for a hundred Mrs. Sticks!

He went back to the others. 'Tea's coming,' he said. 'So cheer up, everyone!'

It wasn't a very cheerful company that sat down to the tea Mrs. Stick brought in. George was now feeling ashamed of her tears. Anne was still upset. Dick tried to make a few silly jokes to cheer everyone up, but they fell so flat that he soon gave it up. Julian was grave and helpful, suddenly very grown-up.

Timothy sat close beside George, his head on her knee. 'I do wish I had a dog who loved me like that,' thought Anne. Timmy kept gazing up at George out of big brown devoted eyes. He had no eyes or ears for anyone but his little mistress now she was sad.

Nobody noticed what they had for tea, but all the same it did them good, and they felt better after it. They didn't like to go out to the beach afterwards in case the telephone bell rang, and there was news of George's mother. So they sat about in the garden, keeping an ear open for the telephone.

From the kitchen came a song.

> '*Georgie-porgie, pudding and pie,*
> *Sat herself down and had a good cry,*
> *Georgie-porgie . . .*'

Julian got up. He went to the kitchen window and looked in. Edgar was there alone.

'Come on out here, Edgar!' said Julian, in a grim voice. 'I'll teach you to sing another song. Come along!'

Edgar didn't stir. 'Can't I sing if I want to?' he said.

'Oh yes,' said Julian, 'but not that song. I'll teach you another. Come along out!'

'No fear,' said Edgar. 'You want to fight me.'

'Yes, I do,' said Julian. 'I think a little bit of good honest fighting would be better for you than sitting singing nasty little songs about a girl who is miserable. Are you coming out? Or shall I come in and fetch you?'

'Ma!' called Edgar, suddenly feeling panicky. 'Ma! Where are you?'

Julian suddenly reached a long arm in at the window, caught hold of Edgar's over-long nose, and pulled it so hard that Edgar yelled in pain.

'Led go! Led go! You're hurding me! Led go by dose!'

Mrs. Stick came hurrying into the kitchen. She gave a scream when she saw what Julian was doing. She flew at him. Julian withdrew his arm, and stood outside the window.

'How dare you!' yelled Mrs. Stick. 'First that girl slaps Edgar, and then you pull his nose! What's the matter with you all?'

'Nothing,' said Julian, pleasantly; 'but there's an awful lot wrong with Edgar, Mrs. Stick. We feel we just *must* put it right. It should be your job, of course, but you don't seem to have done it.'

'You're right down insolent,' said Mrs. Stick, outraged and furious.

'Yes, I dare say I am,' said Julian. 'It's just the effect Edgar has on me. Stinker has the same effect.'

'Stinker!' cried Mrs. Stick, getting angrier still. 'That's not my dog's name, and well you know it.'

'Well, it really ought to be,' said Julian, strolling off. 'Give him a bath, and maybe we'll call him Tinker instead.'

Leaving Mrs. Stick muttering in fury, he went back to the others. They stared at him curiously. He somehow seemed a different Julian – a grim and determined Julian, a very grown-up Julian, a rather frightening Julian.

'I'm afraid the fat's in the fire now,' said Julian, sitting down on the grass. 'I pulled old Edgar's nose nearly off his fat face, and Ma saw me doing it. I guess it's open warfare now! We shan't have a very merry time from now on. I doubt if we'll get any meals.'

'We'll get them ourselves then,' said George. 'I hate Mrs. Stick. I wish Joanna would come back. I hate that horrid Edgar too, and that awful Stinker.'

'Look – there *is* Stinker!' suddenly said Dick, putting out his hand to catch Timothy, who had risen with a growl. But Timmy shook off his hand and leapt across the grass at once. Stinker gave a woeful howl and tried to escape. But Timothy had him by the neck and was shaking him like a rat.

Mrs. Stick appeared with a stick and lashed out, not seeming to mind which dog she hit. Julian rushed for the hose again. Edgar skipped indoors at once, remembering what had happened to him before.

The water gushed out, and Timothy gave a gasp and let go the howling mongrel he held in his teeth. Stinker at once hurled himself on Mrs. Stick, and tried to hide in her skirts trembling with terror.

'I'll poison that dog of yours!' said Mrs. Stick, furiously, to George. 'Always setting on to mine. You look out or I'll poison him.'

She disappeared indoors, and the four children went and sat down again. George looked really alarmed. 'Do you suppose she really *might* try to poison Timmy?' she asked Julian, in a scared voice.

'She's a nasty bit of work,' said Julian, in a low tone. 'I think it would be just as well to keep old Timmy close by us, day and night, and only to feed him ourselves, from our own plates.'

George pulled Timothy to her, horrified at the thought that anyone might want to poison him. But Mrs. Stick really was awful – she might do anything like that, George thought. How she wished her father and mother were back! It was horrid to be on their own, like this.

The telephone bell suddenly shrilled out and made everyone jump. They all leapt to their feet, and Timmy growled. George flew indoors and took down the receiver. She heard her father's voice, and her heart began to beat fast.

'Is that you, George?' said her father. 'Are you all right? I hadn't time to stay and tell you everything.'

'Father – what about Mother? Tell me quick – how is she?' said George.

'We shan't know till the day after next,' said her father. 'I'll telephone tomorrow morning and then the next morning too. I shan't come back till I know she's better.'

'Oh Father – it's awful without you and Mother,' said poor George. 'Mrs. Stick is so horrid.'

'Now, George,' said her father, rather impatiently, 'surely you children can see to yourselves and make do with Mrs. Stick till I get back! Don't worry me about such things now. I've enough worry as it is.'

'When will you be back, do you think?' said George. 'Can I come and see Mother?'

'No,' said her father. 'Not for at least two weeks, they say. I'll be back as soon as I can. But I'm not going to leave your Mother now. She needs me. Good-bye and be good, all of you.'

George put back the receiver. She turned to face the others. 'Shan't know about Mother till the day after next,' she said. 'And we've got to put up with Mrs. Stick till Father comes back – and goodness knows when that will be! It's awful, isn't it?'

Chapter Five

IN THE MIDDLE OF THE NIGHT

Mrs. Stick was in such a bad temper that evening that there was no supper at all. Julian went to ask about some, but he found the kitchen door locked.

He went back to the others with a gloomy face, for they were all hungry. 'She's locked the door,' he said. 'She really is a dreadful creature. I don't believe we'll get any supper tonight.'

'We'll have to wait till she goes to bed,' said George. 'We'll go down and hunt in the larder then, and see what we can find.'

They went to bed hungry. Julian listened for Mrs. Stick and Edgar to go to bed, too. When he heard them going upstairs, and was sure their doors had shut, he slipped down into the kitchen. It was dark there, and Julian was just about to put on the light when he heard the sound of someone breathing heavily. He wondered who it could be. Was it Stinker? No – it couldn't be the dog. It sounded like a human being.

Julian stood there, his hand over the light switch, puzzled and a little scared. It couldn't be a burglar, because burglars don't go to sleep in the house they have come to rob. It couldn't be Mrs. Stick or Edgar. Then who was it?

He snapped on the light. The kitchen was flooded with radiance, and Julian's eyes fastened on the figure of a

small man lying on the sofa. He was fast asleep, his mouth
wide open.

He was not a very pleasant sight. He had not shaved
for some days, and his cheeks and chin were bluish-black.
He didn't seem to have washed for even longer than that,
for his hands were black, and so were his finger-nails. He
had untidy hair, much too long, and a nose exactly like
Edgar's.

'Must be dear Edgar's father,' thought Julian to himself. 'What a sight! Well, poor Edgar hadn't much
chance to be decent with a father and mother like his.'

The man snored. Julian wondered what to do. He
badly wanted to go to the larder, but on the other hand he
didn't particularly want to wake up the man and have a
row. He didn't see how he could turn him out — for all he
knew his aunt and uncle might have agreed to Mrs. Stick's
husband coming there now and again, though he hardly
thought so.

Julian was very hungry. The thought of the good things
in the larder made him snap off the light again and creep
towards the larder door in the dark. He opened the door.
He felt along the shelves. Good! — that felt like a pie of
some sort. He lifted it up and sniffed. It smelt of meat. A
meat-pie — good!

He felt along the shelf again and came to a plate on
which were what he thought must be jam-tarts, for they
were round and flat, and had something sticky in the
middle. Well, a meat-pie and jam-tarts ought to be all
right for four hungry children!

Julian picked up the meat-pie and the dish of tarts,
and made his way carefully out of the larder. He pushed

the door to with his foot. Then he turned to go out of the room.

But in the dark he went the wrong way, and by bad luck walked straight into the sofa! The dish of tarts got a sudden jerk and one of them fell off. It landed on the open mouth of the sleeping man, and woke him up with a start.

'Blow!' said Julian to himself, and began to back away quietly, hoping that the man would turn over and go to sleep again. But the sticky jam-tart sliding down his chin had startled the man, and he sat up with a jerk.

'Who's there? That you, Edgar? What you doing down here?'

Julian said nothing but sidled towards what he hoped was the door. The man leapt up and lurched over to where he thought the light switch was. He found it and switched it on. He stared in the greatest astonishment at Julian.

'What are you doing here?' he demanded.

'Just what I was about to ask *you*,' said Julian, coolly. 'What do you think *you're* doing here, sleeping in my uncle's kitchen?'

'I've a right to be here,' said the man, in a rude voice. 'My wife's cook here, isn't she? My ship's in and I'm on leave. Your uncle arranged with my wife I could come here then, see?'

Julian had feared as much. How awful to have a Mr. Stick as well as a Mrs. and Master Stick in the house! It would be quite unbearable.

'I can ask my uncle about it when he telephones in the morning,' said Julian. 'Now get out of my way, please. I want to go upstairs.'

'Ho!' said Mr. Stick, eyeing the meat-pie and jam-tarts that Julian was carrying. 'Ho! Stealing out of the larder, I see! Nice goings-on I must say.'

Julian was not going to argue with Mr. Stick, who evidently felt that he was top-dog. 'Get out of my way,' he said. 'I will talk to you in the morning after my uncle has telephoned.'

Mr. Stick didn't seem as if he was going to get out of the way at all. He stood there, a nasty little man, not much taller than Julian, a sarcastic smile on his un-shaven face.

Julian pursed up his lips and whistled. There came a bump on the floor above. That was Timothy jumping off George's bed! Then there came the pattering of feet down the stairs and up the kitchen passage. Timmy was coming!

He smelt Mr. Stick in the doorway, put up his hackles, bared his teeth and growled. Mr. Stick hastily removed himself from the doorway and then neatly banged the door in the dog's face. He grinned at Julian.

'Now what are you going to do?' he said.

'Shall I tell you?' said Julian, his temper suddenly rising. 'I'm going to hurl this nice juicy meat-pie straight into your grinning face!'

He raised his arm, and Mr. Stick ducked.

'Now don't you do that,' he said. 'I'm only pulling your leg, see? Don't you waste that nice meat-pie. You can go upstairs if you want to.'

He moved away to the sofa. Julian opened the door and Timothy bounded in growling. Mr. Stick eyed him uncomfortably.

'Don't you let that nasty great dog come near me,' he said. 'I don't like dogs.'

'Then I wonder you don't get rid of Stinker,' said Julian. 'Come here, Timmy! Leave him alone. He's not worth growling at.'

Julian went upstairs with Timothy close at his heels. The others crowded round him, wondering what had happened, for they had heard the voices downstairs. They laughed when Julian told them how he had nearly thrown the meat-pie at Mr. Stick.

'It would have served him right,' said Anne, 'though

it would have been a great pity, because we shouldn't have been able to eat it. Well, Mrs. Stick may be simply horrible, but she *can* cook. This pie is gorgeous.'

The children finished all the pie and the tarts, too. Julian told them all about Mr. Stick coming on leave from his ship.

'Three Sticks are a lot too much,' said Dick thoughtfully. 'Pity we can't get rid of them all and manage for ourselves. George, can't you possibly persuade your father tomorrow to let us get rid of the Sticks and look after ourselves?'

'I'll try,' said George. 'But you know what he is – awfully difficult to argue with. But I'll try. Golly, I'm sleepy now. Come on, Timmy, let's get to bed! Lie on my feet. I'm hardly going to let you out of my sight now, in case those awful Sticks poison you!'

Soon the four children, now no longer hungry, were sleeping peacefully. They did not fear the Sticks coming up to their rooms, for they knew that Timmy would wake and warn them at once. Timmy was the best guard they could have.

In the morning Mrs. Stick actually produced some sort of breakfast, which surprised the children very much. 'Guess she knows your father will telephone, George,' said Julian, 'and she wants to keep herself in the right. When did he say he would 'phone? Nine o'clock, wasn't it? Well, it's half-past eight now. Let's go for a quick run down to the beach and back.'

So off they went, the five of them, ignoring Edgar, who stood in the back garden ready to make some of his silly faces at them. The children couldn't help thinking

he must be a bit mad. He didn't behave at all like a boy
of Julian's age.

When they came back it was about ten minutes to nine.
'We'll sit in the sitting-room till the telephone rings,' said
Julian. 'We don't want Mrs. Stick to answer it first.'

But to their great dismay, as they reached the house,
they heard Mrs. Stick using the telephone in the hall!

'Yes, sir,' they heard her say, 'everything is quite all right.
I can manage the children, sir, even if they do make things
a bit difficult. Yes, sir. Of course, sir. Well, sir, it's lucky
my husband is home on leave from his ship, sir, because
he can help me round, like, and it makes things easier.
Don't you worry about nothing, sir, and don't you bother
to come back till you're ready. I'll manage everything.'

George flew into the hall like a wild thing, and
snatched the receiver out of Mrs. Stick's hand.

'Father! It's me, George! How's Mother? Tell me
quick!'

'No worse, George,' said her father's voice. 'But we
shan't know anything definite till tomorrow morning.
I'm glad to hear from Mrs. Stick that everything is all
right. I'm very upset and worried, and I'm glad to feel I
can tell your Mother that you are all right, and everything is going smoothly at Kirrin Cottage.'

'But it isn't,' said George, wildly. 'It isn't. It's all
horrid. Can't the Sticks go and let us manage things by
ourselves?'

'Good gracious me, of course not,' said her father's
voice, surprised and annoyed. 'What can you be thinking of? I did hope, George, that you would be sensible
and helpful. I must say . . .'

'*You* talk to him, Julian,' said George, helplessly, and thrust the receiver into Julian's hand. The boy put it to his ear and spoke into the telephone in his clear voice

'Good morning, sir. This is Julian! I'm glad my aunt is no worse.'

'Well, she will be if she thinks things are going wrong at Kirrin Cottage,' said Uncle Quentin, in an exasperated voice. 'Can't you manage George and make her see reason? Good gracious, can't she put up with the Sticks for a week or two? I tell you frankly, Julian, I am not going to sack the Sticks in my absence — I want the house ready for me to bring back your aunt. If you can't put up with them, you had better find out from your own parents if they can take you back for the rest of the holidays. But George is not to go with you. She is to stay at Kirrin Cottage. That's my last word on the subject.'

'But, sir,' began Julian, wondering how in the world he could deal properly with his hot-tempered uncle, 'I must tell you that . . .'

There was a click at the other end of the 'phone. Uncle Quentin had put down his receiver and gone. There was no more to be said. Blow! Julian pursed up his mouth and looked round at the others, frowning.

'He's gone!' he said. 'Cut me off just as I was trying to reason with him.'

'Serves you right!' said Mrs. Stick's harsh voice from the end of the hall. 'Now you know where you stand. I'm here and I'm staying here, on your uncle's orders. And you're all going to behave yourselves, or it'll be the worse for you.'

Chapter Six

JULIAN DEFEATS THE STICKS

THERE was a slam. The kitchen door shut, and Mrs. Stick could be heard telling the news triumphantly to Edgar and Mr. Stick. The children went into the sitting-room, sat down and stared at one another gloomily.

'Father's awful!' said George, furiously. 'He never will listen to anything.'

'Well, after all, he is very upset,' said Dick, reasonably. 'It was a great pity that he rang before nine, so that Mrs. Stick got her say in first.'

'What did Father say to you?' said George. 'Tell us exactly.'

'He said that if we couldn't put up with the Sticks, Anne and Dick and I were to go back to our own parents,' said Julian. 'But you were to stay here.'

George stared at Julian. 'Well,' she said at last, 'you *can't* put up with the Sticks, so you'd better all go back. I can look after myself.'

'Don't be an idiot!' said Julian, giving her arm a friendly shake, 'You know we wouldn't desert you. I can't say I look forward to the idea of being under the thumb of the amiable Sticks for a week or two, but there are worse things than that. We'll "stick" it together.'

But the feeble little joke didn't raise a smile, even from Anne. The idea of being under the Sticks' three thumbs was a most unpleasant prospect. Timothy put his head on

George's knee. She patted him and looked round.

'You go back home,' she said to the others. 'I've got a plan of my own, and you're not in it. I've got Timmy, and he'll look after me. Telephone to your parents and go home tomorrow.'

George stared round defiantly. Her head was up, and there was no doubt but that she had made a plan of some sort.

Julian felt uneasy.

'Don't be silly,' he said. 'I tell you we all stand together in this. If you've got a plan, we'll come into it. But we're staying here with you, whatever happens.'

'Stay if you like,' said George, 'but my plan goes on, and you'll find you'll have to go home in the end. Come on, Timothy! Let's go to Jim and see if my boat is ready.'

'We'll go with you,' said Dick. He was sorry for George. He could see below her defiance, and he knew she was very unhappy, worried about her mother, angry with her father, and upset because she felt the others were staying on because of her, when they could go back home and have a lovely time.

It was not a happy day. George was very stand-offish, and kept on insisting that the others should go back home and leave her. She grew quite angry when they were as insistent that they would not.

'You're spoiling my plan,' she said at last. 'You *might* go back, you really might. I tell you, you're spoiling my plan completely.'

'Well, what *is* your plan?' said Julian impatiently. 'I can't help feeling you're just *pretending* you've got a plan so that we'll go.'

'I'm *not* pretending,' said George, losing her temper. 'Do I ever pretend? You know I don't! If I say I've got a plan, I *have* got a plan. But I'm not giving it away, so it's no good asking me. It's my own secret, private plan.'

'Well, I really do think you might tell us,' said Dick, quite hurt. 'After all, we're your best friends, aren't we? And we're going to stick by you, plan or no plan – yes, even if we spoil your plan, as you say, we shall still stay here with you.'

'I shan't *let* you spoil my plan,' said George, her eyes flashing. 'You're mean. You're against me, just like the Sticks are.'

'Oh, George, don't,' said Anne, almost in tears. 'Don't let's quarrel. It's bad enough quarrelling with those awful Sticks, without *us* quarrelling too.'

George's temper died down as quickly as it had risen. She looked ashamed.

'Sorry!' she said. 'I'm an idiot. I won't quarrel. But I do mean what I say. I shall go on with my plan, and I shan't tell you what it is, because if I do, it will spoil the holidays for you. Please believe me.'

'Let's take our dinner out with us again,' said Julian, getting up. 'We'll all feel better away from this house to-day. I'll go and tackle the old Stick.'

'Dear old Ju, isn't he brave!' said Anne, who would rather have died than go and face Mrs. Stick at that moment.

Mrs. Stick proved very difficult. She felt rather victorious at the time, and was also very annoyed to find that her beautiful meat-pie and jam-tarts had disappeared. Mr. Stick was in the middle of telling her where they had gone when Julian appeared.

'How you can expect sandwiches for a picnic when you've stolen my meat-pie and jam-tarts, I *don't* know!' she began, indignantly. 'You can have dry bread and jam for your picnic, and that's all. And what's more, I wouldn't give you that either except that I'm glad to be rid of you.'

'Good riddance to bad rubbish,' murmured Edgar to himself. He was lying sprawled on the sofa, reading some kind of highly-coloured comic paper.

'If you've anything to say to me, Edgar, come outside and say it,' said Julian, dangerously.

'You leave Edgar alone,' said Mrs. Stick, at once.

'There's nothing I should like better,' said Julian, scornfully. 'Who wants to be with him? Cowardly little spotty-face!'

'Now, now, look 'ere!' began Mr. Stick, from his corner.

'I don't want to look at you,' said Julian at once.

'Now, look *'ere*,' said Mr. Stick, angrily, standing up.

'I've told you I don't want to,' said Julian. 'You're not a pleasant sight.'

'*Insolence!*' said Mrs. Stick, rapidly losing her temper.

'No, not insolence – just the plain truth,' said Julian, airily. Mrs. Stick glared at him. Julian defeated her. He had such a ready tongue, and he said everything so politely. The ruder his words were, the more politely he spoke. Mrs. Stick didn't understand people like Julian. She felt that they were too clever for her. She hated the boy, and banged a saucepan viciously down on the sink, wishing that it was Julian's head under the saucepan instead of the sink.

Stinker jumped up and growled at the sudden noise.

'Hallo, Stinker!' said Julian. 'Had a bath yet? Alas, no! – as smelly as ever, aren't you?'

'You know that dog's name isn't Stinker,' said Mrs. Stick, angrily. 'You get out of my kitchen.'

'Right!' said Julian. 'Pleased to go. Don't bother about the dry bread and jam. I'll manage something a bit better than that.'

He went out, whistling. Stinker growled, and Edgar repeated loudly what he had said before: 'Good riddance to bad rubbish!'

'What did you say?' said Julian, suddenly poking his head in at the kitchen door again. But Edgar did not dare to repeat it, so off went Julian again, whistling merrily, but not feeling nearly as merry as his whistle. He was worried. After all, if Mrs. Stick was going to make meals as difficult as this, life was not going to be very pleasant at Kirrin Cottage.

'Anyone feel inclined to have dry bread and jam for lunch?' inquired Julian, when he returned to the others. 'Not? I rather thought so, so I turned down Mrs. Stick's kind offer. I vote we go and buy something decent. That shop in the village has good sausage-rolls.'

George was very silent all that day. She was worrying about her mother, the others knew. She was probably thinking about her plan too, they thought, and wondered whatever it could be.

'Shall we go over to Kirrin Island today?' asked Julian,

thinking that it would take George's mind off her worries, if they went to her beloved island.

George shook her head.

'No,' she said. 'I don't feel like it. The boat's all ready, I know – but I just don't feel like it. You see, till I know Mother is going to get better, I don't feel I want to be out of reach of the house. If a telephone message came from Father, the Sticks could always send Edgar to look for me – and if I was on the island, he couldn't find me.'

The children messed about that day, doing nothing at all. They went back to tea, and Mrs. Stick provided them with bread and butter and jam, but no cake. The milk was sour too, and everyone had to have tea without milk, which they all disliked.

As they ate their tea, the children heard Edgar outside the window. He held a tin bowl in his hand, and put it down on the grass outside.

'Your dog's dinner,' he yelled.

'He looks like a dog's dinner himself,' said Dick, in disgust. 'Messy creature!'

That made everyone laugh. 'Edgar, the Dog's Dinner!' said Anne. 'Any biscuits in that tin on the sideboard, do you think, George?'

George got up to see. Timothy slipped out of doors and went to the dish put down for him. He sniffed at it. George, coming back from the sideboard, looked out of the window as she passed and saw him. At once the thought of poison came back to her mind and she yelled to Timothy, making the others jump out of their skins.

'Tɪᴍ! Tɪᴍ! Don't touch it!'

Timothy wagged his tail as if to say he didn't mean to

touch it, anyway. George rushed out of doors, and picked up the mess of raw meat. She sniffed at it.

'You haven't touched it, have you, Timothy?' she said, anxiously.

Dick leaned out of the window.

'No, he didn't eat any. I watched him. He sniffed all round and about it, but he wouldn't touch it. I bet it's been dosed with rat-poison or something.'

George was very white. 'Oh Timmy!' she said. 'You're such a sensible dog. You wouldn't touch poisoned stuff, would you?'

'Woof!' said Timmy, decidedly. Stinker heard the bark and put his nose out of the kitchen door.

George called to him in a loud voice:

'Stinker, Stinker, come here! Timmy doesn't want his dinner. You can have it. Come along, Stinker, here it is!'

Edgar came rushing out behind Stinker. 'Don't you give that to him,' he said.

'Why not?' asked George. 'Go on, Edgar – tell me why not.'

'He don't eat raw meat,' said Edgar, after a pause. 'He only eats dog biscuits.'

'That's a lie!' said George, flaming up. 'I saw him eating meat yesterday. Here, Stinker – you come and eat this.'

Edgar snatched the bowl from George, almost snarling at her, and ran indoors at top speed. George was about to go after him, but Julian, who had jumped out of the window when Edgar came up, stopped her.

'No good, old thing!' he said. 'You won't get anything out of him. The meat's probably at the back of the kitchen

fire by now. From now on, we feed Timothy ourselves with meat bought from the butcher with our own money. Don't be afraid that he'll eat poisoned stuff. He's too wise a dog for that.'

'He might, if he was terribly, awfully hungry, Julian,' said George, looking rather green now. She felt sick inside. 'I wasn't going to let Stinker eat that poisoned stuff, of course, but I guessed that if it *was* poisoned, one of the Sticks would come rushing out and stop Stinker eating it. And Edgar did. So it proves it was poisoned, doesn't it?'

'I rather think it does,' said Julian. 'But don't worry, George. Timmy won't be poisoned.'

'But he might, he might,' said George, putting her hand on the big dog's head. 'Oh, I can't bear the thought of it, Julian. I can't, I really can't.'

'Don't think about it then,' said Julian, taking her indoors again. 'Here, have a biscuit!'

'You don't think the Sticks would poison *us*, do you?' said Anne, looking suddenly scared and gazing at her biscuit as if it might bite her.

'No, idiot. They only want to get Timmy out of the way because he guards us so well,' said Julian. 'Don't look so scared. All this will settle down in a day or two, and we'll have a grand time after all. You'll see!'

But Julian only said this to comfort his little sister. Secretly he was very worried. He wished he could take Anne, Dick and George back to his own home. But he knew George wouldn't come. And how could they leave her to the Sticks? It was quite impossible. Friends must stick together, and somehow they must face things until Aunt Fanny and Uncle Quentin came back.

Chapter Seven

BETTER NEWS

'Do you think we'd better slip down after the Sticks have gone to bed and get some food out of the larder again?' said Dick, when no supper appeared that evening.

Julian didn't feel inclined to sneak down and confront Mr. Stick again. Not that he was afraid of him, but the whole thing was so unpleasant. This was their house, the food was theirs – so why should they have to beg for it, or take it on the sly? It was ridiculous.

'Come here, Timothy!' said Julian. The dog left George's side and went to Julian, looking up at the boy inquiringly. 'You're going to come with me and persuade dear kind Mrs. Stick to give us the best things out of the larder!' said Julian, with a grin.

The others laughed, cheering up at once.

'Good idea!' said Dick. 'Can we all come and see the fun.'

'Better not,' said Julian. 'I can manage fine by myself.'

He went down the passage to the kitchen. The wireless was going inside, so no one in the kitchen heard Julian till he was actually standing inside the door. Then Edgar looked up and saw Timothy as well as Julian.

Edgar was scared of the big dog, who was now growling fiercely. He went behind the kitchen sofa and stayed there, eyeing Timmy fearfully.

'What do you want?' said Mrs. Stick, turning off the wireless.

'Supper,' said Julian, pleasantly. 'Supper! The best things out of the larder – bought with my uncle's money, cooked on my aunt's stove with gas she pays for – yes, supper! Open the larder door and let's see what there is in there.'

'Well, of all the nerve!' began Mr. Stick, in an amazed voice.

'You can have a loaf of bread and some cheese,' said Mrs. Stick, 'and that's my last word.'

'Well, it isn't my last word,' said Julian, and he went to the larder door. 'Timmy, keep to heel! Growl all you like, but don't bite anybody – yet!'

Timmy's growls were really frightful. Even Mr. Stick put himself at the other end of the room. As for Stinker, he was nowhere to be seen. He had gone into the scullery at the very first growl, and was now shivering behind the wringer.

Mrs. Stick's mouth went into a hard straight line. 'You take the bread and cheese and clear out,' she said.

Julian opened the larder door, whistling softly, which annoyed Mrs. Stick more than anything else. 'My word!' said Julian, admiringly. 'You do know how to stock a larder, I must say, Mrs. Stick. A roast chicken! I thought I smelt one cooking. I suppose Mr. Stick killed one of our chickens today. I thought I heard a lot of squawking. And what fine tomatoes! Best to be got from the village, I've no doubt. And oh, Mrs. *Stick* – what a perfectly *marvellous* treacle tart! I must say you're a good cook, I really must!'

Julian picked up the chicken, the dish of tomatoes, and then balanced the plate with the treacle tart on the top.

Mrs. Stick yelled at him.

'You leave them things alone! That's our supper! You leave them there.'

'You've made a little mistake,' said Julian, politely. 'It's *our* supper! We've had very little to eat today, and we could do with a good supper. Thanks awfully!'

'Now look 'ere!' began Mr. Stick, angrily, furious at seeing his lovely supper walking away.

'You surely don't want me to look at you *again*,' said Julian, in a tone of amazement. 'What for? Have you shaved yet – or washed? I'm afraid not. So, if you don't mind I think I'd rather *not* look at you.'

Mr. Stick was speechless. He was not ready with his tongue at any time, and a boy like Julian took his breath away, and left him with nothing to say except his favourite 'Now, look 'ere!'

'Put them things down,' said Mrs. Stick sharply. 'What do you think we're going to have for *our* supper if you walk off with them; you tell me that!'

'Easy!' said Julian. 'Let me offer you *our* supper – bread and cheese, Mrs. Stick, bread and cheese!'

Mrs. Stick made an angry noise, and started to go after Julian, her hand raised. But Timothy immediately leapt at her, and his teeth snapped together with a loud click.

'Oh!' howled Mrs. Stick. 'That dog of yours nearly took my hand off! The brute! I'll do for him one day, you see if I don't.'

'You had a good try today, didn't you?' said Julian, in a quiet voice, fixing his eyes straight on the woman's face. 'That's a matter for the police, isn't it? Be careful, Mrs. Stick. I've a good mind to go to the police tomorrow.'

Just as before, the mention of the police seemed to frighten Mrs. Stick. She cast a look at her husband and took a step backward. Julian wondered if the man had done something wrong and was hiding from the police. He never seemed to put a foot out of doors.

The boy went up the passage triumphantly. Timmy followed at his heels, disappointed that he hadn't been able to get a nibble at Stinker. Julian marched into the sitting-room, and set the dishes carefully down on the table.

'What ho!' he said. 'Look what *I've* got – the Sticks'

own supper!' Then he told the others all that had happened, and they laughed loudly.

'How do you think of all those things to say?' said
Anne, admiringly. 'I don't wonder you make them feel
wild, Ju. It's a good thing we've got Timmy to back us
up.'

'Yes. I shouldn't feel nearly so bold without Timmy,'
said Julian.

It was a very good supper. There were knives and forks
in the sideboard, and the children made do with fruit
plates from the sideboard too, rather than go and get
plates from the kitchen. There was bread over from their
tea, so they were able to make a very good meal, They
enjoyed it thoroughly.

'Sorry we can't give you the chicken bones, Tim,' said
George. 'But they might split inside you and injure you.
You can have all the scraps. See you don't leave any for
Stinker!'

Timmy didn't. With two or three great gulps he cleared
his plate, and then sat waiting for any scraps of treacle
tart that might descend his way.

The children felt cheerful after such a good meal. They
had completely eaten the chicken. Nothing was left except a pile of bones. They had eaten all the tomatoes too,
finished the bread, and enjoyed every scrap of the treacle
tart.

It was late. Anne yawned, and then George yawned
too. 'Let's go to bed,' she said. 'I don't feel like having a
game of cards or anything.'

So they went to bed, and as usual Timothy lay heavily
on George's feet. He lay there awake for some time, his

ears cocked to hear noises from below. He heard the
Sticks go up to bed. He heard doors closing. He heard a
whine from Stinker. Then all was silence. Timmy dropped
his head on to his paws and slept – but he kept one ear
cocked for danger. Timothy didn't trust the Sticks any
more than the children did!

The children awoke very early in the morning. Julian
awoke first. It was a marvellous day. Julian went to the
window and looked out. The sky was a very pale blue, and
rosy-pink clouds floated about it. The sea was a clean blue
too, smooth and calm. Julian remembered what Anne
often said – she said that the world in the early morning
always looked as if it had come back fresh from the
laundry – so clean and new and fresh!

The children all bathed before breakfast, and this time
they were back at half-past eight, afraid that George's
father might telephone early again. Julian saw Mrs.
Stick on the stairs and called to her.

'Has my uncle telephoned yet?'

'No,' said the woman, in a surly tone. She had been
hoping that the telephone would ring whilst the children
were out, then, as she had done the day before, she could
answer it, and get a few words in first.

'We'll have breakfast now, please,' said Julian. 'A
good breakfast, Mrs. Stick. My uncle *might* ask us what
we'd had for breakfast, mightn't he? You never know.'

Mrs. Stick evidently thought that Julian might tell his
uncle if she gave them only bread and butter for breakfast, so very soon the children smelt a delicious smell of
bacon frying. Mrs. Stick brought in a dish of it garnished
with tomatoes. She banged it down on the table with the

plates. Edgar arrived with a pot of tea and a tray of cups and saucers.

'Ah, here is dear Edgar!' said Julian, in a tone of amiable surprise. 'Dear old spotty-face!'

'Garn!' said Edgar, and banged down the teapot. Timmy growled, and Edgar fled for his life.

George didn't want any breakfast. Julian put hers back in the warm dish and put a plate over it. He knew that she was waiting for news. If only the telephone would ring – then she would know if her mother was really better or not.

It did ring as they were halfway through the meal. George was there before the bell had stopped pealing. She put the receiver to her ear. 'Father! Yes, it's George. How's Mother?'

There was a pause as George listened. All the children stopped eating and listened in silence, waiting for George to speak. They would know by her next words if the news was good or not.

'Oh – oh, I'm so glad!' they heard George say. 'Did she have the operation yesterday? Oh, you never told me! But it's all right now, is it? Poor Mother! Give her my love. I do want to see her. Oh Father, can't I come?'

Evidently the answer was no. George listened for a while, then spoke a few more words and said good-bye.

She ran into the sitting-room. 'You heard, didn't you?' she said, joyfully. 'Mother's better. She'll get all right now, and will be back home soon – in about ten days. Father won't come back till he brings her home. It's good news about Mother – but I'm afraid we can't get rid of the Sticks.'

Chapter Eight

GEORGE'S PLAN

Mrs. Stick had overheard the conversation on the telephone – at least, she had heard George's side of it. She knew that George's mother was better and that her father would not return till her mother could be brought home. That would be in about ten days! The Sticks could have a fine time till then, no doubt about that!

George suddenly found that her appetite had come back. She ate her bacon hungrily, and scraped the dish round with a piece of bread. She had three cups of tea, and then sat back contentedly.

'I feel better,' she said. Anne slipped her hand in hers. She was very glad that her aunt was going to be all right. If it wasn't for those awful Sticks they could have a lovely time. Then George said something that made Julian cross.

'Well, now that I know Mother is going to be better, I can stand up to the Sticks all right by myself with Timmy. So I want you three to go back home and finish the hols. without me. I shall be all right.'

'Shut up, George,' said Julian. 'We've argued this all out before. I've made up my mind – and I don't change it, any more than *you* do, when I've made it up. You make me cross.'

'Well,' said George, 'I told you I'd got a plan – and you don't come into it, I'm afraid – and you'll find you'll have to go back home whether you mean to or not.'

'Don't be so mysterious, George!' said Julian, impatiently. 'What is this strange plan? You'd better tell us,
even if we're not in it. Can't you trust us?'

'Yes, of course. But you might try to stop me,' said
George, looking sulky.

'Then you'd certainly better tell us,' said Julian feeling uneasy. George was such a madcap once she got ideas
into her head. Goodness knows what she might do!

But George wouldn't say another word. Julian gave it
up at last, but secretly made up his mind not to let George
out of his sight that day. If she was going to carry out some
wild plan, then she would have to do it under Julian's
eye!

But George didn't seem to be carrying out any wild
plan. She bathed again with the others, went for a walk
with them, and went for a row on the sea. She didn't
want to go to Kirrin Island, so the others didn't press her,
thinking that she didn't want to be out of sight of the
beach in case Edgar came with a message from her
father.

It was quite a pleasant day. The children bought saus-
age rolls again, and fruit, and picnicked on the beach.
Timmy had a large and juicy bone from the butcher's.

'I've got a bit of shopping to do,' said George, about
tea-time. 'You others go and see if Mrs. Stick is getting
some tea for us, and I'll fly down to the shops and get
what I want.'

Julian pricked up his ears at once. Was George sending them off so that she could be alone to carry out this
mysterious plan of hers?

'I'll come with you,' said Julian, getting up. 'Dick can

ackle Mrs. Stick for once, and take Timmy with him.'

'No, you go,' said George. 'I won't be long.'

But Julian was determined not to go. In the end they
all went with George, for Dick did not want to face Mrs.
Stick without Julian or George.

George went into the little general shop and got a new
battery for her torch. She bought two boxes of matches,
and a bottle of methylated spirit.

'Whatever do you want that for?' said Anne in surprise.

'Oh, it might come in useful,' said George, and said
no more.

They all went back to Kirrin Cottage. Tea was actuall
on the table! True, it was not a thrilling tea, being merel
bread and jam and a pot of hot tea – still it was there, an
was eatable.

It rained that evening. The children sat round th
table and played cards. Their hearts were lighter no
that they had had good news of George's mother. In th
middle of the game Julian got up and rang the bel
The others stared at him in the greatest surprise.

'What are you ringing the bell for?' asked George, he
eyes wide with astonishment.

'To tell Mrs. Stick to bring some supper,' said Julia
with a grin. But no one answered the bell. So Julian ran
again and then again.

The kitchen door opened at last and Mrs. Stick cam
up the passage, evidently in a bad temper. She came int
the sitting-room.

'You stop ringing that bell!' she said, angrily. 'I'm n
answering any bells rung by you.'

'I rang it to tell you that we wanted some supper,' sai
Julian, 'And to say that if you would rather I came an
got it myself from the larder – with Timmy – as I did la
night, I'll come with pleasure. But if not, you can bring
decent supper to us yourself.'

'If you come stealing things out of my larder agai
I'll – I'll . . .' began Mrs. Stick.

'You'll call in the police!' Julian finished for her. 'D
That would please us very much. I can see our local polic
man taking down all the details in his notebook. I cou
give him quite a few.'

Mrs. Stick muttered something rude under her breat]

glared at Julian as if she could kill him, and went off
down the passage again. By the sound of the clattering
and crashing of crockery in the kitchen it was plain that
Mrs. Stick was getting some sort of supper for them, and
Julian grinned to himself as he dealt out the cards.

Supper was not as good as the night before, but it was
not bad. It was a little cold ham, cheese and the remains
of a milk pudding. There was also a plate of cooked meat
for Timmy.

George looked at it sharply. 'Take that away,' she
said. 'I bet you've poisoned it again. Take it away!'

'No. On the contrary, leave it here,' said Julian. 'I'll
take it down to the local chemist tomorrow and get him
to test it. If, as George thinks, it's poisoned, the chemist
might have a lot of interesting things to tell us.'

Mrs. Stick took the meat away without a word. 'Hor-
ible woman!' said George, pulling Timothy close to her.
'How I hate her! I feel so afraid for Timmy.'

Somehow that spoilt the evening. As it grew dark the
children became sleepy. 'It's ten o'clock,' said Julian.
'Bed, I think, everyone! Anne ought to have gone long
ago. She isn't nearly old enough to stay up as late as this.'

'*Well!*' began Anne, indignantly. 'I'm nearly as old
as George, aren't I? I can't help being younger, can I?'

'All right, all right!' said Julian laughing. 'I shan't
make you go off to bed by yourself, don't worry. We all
keep together in this house whilst the Sticks are about.
Come on! We'll go now, shall we?'

The children were tired. They had swum, walked and
rowed that day. Julian tried to keep awake a little while,
but he too fell asleep very quickly.

He awoke with a jump, thinking that he had heard
noise. But everything was quiet. What could the nois
have been? Was it one of the Sticks creeping about
No – it couldn't be that, or Tim would have barked th
house down. Then what was it? *Some*-thing must hav
waked him.

'I suppose it's not old George doing anything abou
that plan of hers!' thought Julian, suddenly. He sat up
He felt about for his dressing-gown and put it on. With
out waking Dick he crept to the girls' room, and switche
on his torch to see that they were all right.

Anne was in her bed, sleeping peacefully. But George'
bed was empty. George's clothes were gone!

'Blow!' said Julian, under his breath. 'Where has sh
gone? I bet she's run away to find where her mothe
is!'

His torch picked out a white envelope pinned t
George's pillow. He stepped softly over to it.

It had his name printed on it in bold letters. 'JULIAN.
Julian ripped it open and read it.

'Dear JULIAN,' said the note,

'Don't be angry with me, please. I daren't stay i
Kirrin Cottage any longer in case the Sticks somehow
poison Timmy. You know that would break my heart
So I've gone to live by myself on our island til
Mother and Father come back. Please leave a note fo
Father and tell him to ask Jim to sail near Kirrin Islanc
with his little red flag flying from the mast as soon a
they are back. Then I'll come home. You and Dick anc
Anne must go back to your own parents now I've gone

It would be silly to stay at Kirrin Cottage with the
Sticks now I'm not there.

Love from
GEORGE.'

Julian read the note through. 'Well, why didn't I *guess*
that was her plan!' he said to himself. 'That's why we
didn't come into it! She meant to go off by herself with
Timmy. I can't let her do that. She can't live all by herself on Kirrin Island for so long. She might fall ill. She
might slip on a rock and hurt herself, and no one would
ever know!'

The boy was really worried about the determined
little girl. He wondered what to do. That noise he
heard must have been made by George. So she couldn't
have got a very long start really. If he tore down to the
beach, George might still be there, and he could stop
her.

So, in his dressing-gown, he ran down the front path,
out of the gate, and took the road to the beach. The rain
had stopped, and the stars were out. But it was not at all
a light night.

'How can George expect to get through those rocks in
the dark,' he thought. 'She's mad! She'll strike her boat
on a rock, and sink.'

He tore on in the darkness, talking aloud to himself.
'No wonder she wanted a new battery for her torch, and
matches – and I suppose the methylated spirit was for her
little cooking stove! Why ever couldn't she tell us? It
would have been fun to go with her.'

He came to the beach. He saw the light of a torch

where George kept her boat. He ran to it, his feet sinking in the soft wet sand.

'George! Idiot! You're not to go off like this all alone in the dead of night!' called Julian.

George was pushing her boat out into the water. She jumped when she heard Julian's voice. 'You can't stop me!' she said. 'I'm just off!'

But Julian caught hold of the boat, as he waded up to his waist in the water. 'George, listen to me! You can't go like this. You'll strike a rock. Come back!'

'No,' said George, getting cross. 'You can go back to your own home, Julian. I shall be all right. Let go my boat!'

'George, why didn't you tell me your plan?' said Julian, almost swept off his feet by a wave. 'Dash these waves! I shall have to get into the boat.'

He climbed in. He could not see George, but he felt quite certain she was glaring at him. Timmy licked his wet legs.

'You're spoiling everything,' said George, with a break in her voice that meant she was upset.

'I'm not, silly!' said Julian, in a gentle voice. 'Listen! - you come back to Kirrin Cottage with me now, George! And I'll faithfully promise you something. Tomorrow we'll *all* go to the island with you. See? The whole lot of us. Why shouldn't we? Your mother said we could spend a week there, anyway, didn't she? We shall be out of the reach of those horrible Sticks. We shall enjoy ourselves and have a marvellous time. So will you come back now, George, and let us go together tomorrow?'

Chapter Nine

AN EXCITING NIGHT

THERE was a silence, except for the waves splashing round the boat. Then George's voice came out of the darkness, lifted joyfully.

'Oh Julian – do you really mean it? Will you really come with me? I was afraid I'd get into trouble for doing this, because Father said I must stay at Kirrin Cottage till he came back – and you know how he hates disobedience. But I knew if I stayed there, you would too – and I didn't want you to be miserable with those horrid Sticks – so I thought I'd come away. I didn't think you'd come too, because of getting into trouble! I never even thought of asking you.'

'You're a very stupid person sometimes, aren't you, George?' said Julian. 'As if we'd care about getting into trouble, so long as we were all together, sticking by one another! Of course we'll come with you – and I'll take all the responsibility for this escape, and tell your father it's my fault.'

'Oh no you won't,' said George, quickly. 'I shall say it was my idea. If I do wrong, I'm not afraid to own up to it. You know that.'

'Well, we won't argue that now,' said Julian. 'We shall have at least a week or ten days on Kirrin Island to do all the arguing we want to. The thing is – let's get back now, wake up the others for a bit, and have a nice quiet

talk in the dead of night about this plan of yours. I must
say it's a very, very good idea!'

George was overjoyed. 'I feel as if I could hug you
Julian,' she said. 'Where are the oars? Oh, here they
are! The boat's floated quite a long way out.'

She rowed strongly back to the shore. Julian jumped
out and pulled the boat up the beach, with George's help.
He shone his torch into the boat and gave an exclamation.

'You've quite a nice little store of things here,' he said.
'Bread and ham and butter and stuff. How did you manage to get them without old Mr. Stick seeing you tonight?
I suppose you slipped down and got them out of the
larder?'

'Yes, I did,' said George. 'But there was no one in the
kitchen tonight. Perhaps Mr. Stick has gone to sleep upstairs. Or maybe he has gone back to his ship. Anyway
there was no one there when I crept down, not even
Stinker.'

'We'd better leave them here,' said Julian. 'Stuff them
into that locker and shut down the lid. No one will guess
there's anything there. We'll have to bring down a lot more
stuff if we're all going to live on the island. Golly, this is
going to be fun!'

The children made their way back to the house, feeling
thrilled and excited. Julian's wet dressing-gown flapped
round his legs, and he pulled it up high to be out of the
way. Timothy gambolled round, not seeming at all surprised at the night's doings.

When they got back to the house they woke the other
two, who listened in astonishment to what had happened
that night. Anne was so excited to think that they were

all going to live on the island that she raised her voice in joy.

'Oh! That's the loveliest thing that could happen! Oh, I do think . . .'

'Shut up!' said three furious voices in loud whispers. 'You'll wake the Sticks!'

'Sorry!' whispered Anne. 'But oh – it's so terribly, awfully exciting.'

They began to discuss their plans. 'If we go for a week or ten days, we must take plenty of stores,' said Julian. 'The thing is – can we possibly find food enough for so long? Even if we entirely empty the larder I doubt if that would be enough for a week or so. We all seem such hungry people, somehow.'

'Julian,' said George, suddenly remembering something, '*I* know what we'll do! Mother has a store-cupboard in her room. She keeps dozens and dozens of tins of food there, in case we ever get snowed up in the winter, and can't get to the village. That has happened once or twice you know. And I know where Mother keeps the key! Can't we open the cupboard and get out some tins?'

'Of course!' said Julian, delighted. 'I know Aunt Fanny wouldn't mind. And anyway, we can make a list of what we take and replace them for her, if she does mind. It will be my birthday soon, and I am sure to get money then.'

'Where's the key?' whispered Dick.

'Let's go into Mother's room, and I'll show you where she keeps it,' said George. 'I only hope she hasn't taken it with her.'

But George's mother had felt far too ill when she left home to think of cupboard keys. George fumbled at the back of a drawer in the dressing-table and brought out two or three keys tied together with thin string. She fitted first one and then another into a cupboard set in the wall. The second one opened the door.

Julian shone his torch into the cupboard. It was filled with tins of food of all kinds, neatly arranged on the shelves.

'Golly!' said Dick, his eyes gleaming. 'Soup – tins of meat – tins of fruit – tinned milk – sardines – tinned butter – biscuits – tinned vegetables! There's everything we want here!'

'Yes,' said Julian, pleased. 'It's fine. We'll take all we can carry. Is there a sack or two anywhere about, George, do you know?'

Soon the tins were quietly packed into two sacks. The cupboard door was shut and locked again. The children stole to their own rooms once more.

'Well, that's the biggest problem solved – food,' said Julian. 'We'll raid the larder too, and take what bread there is – and cake. What about water, George? Is there any on the island?'

'Well, I suppose there is some in that old well,' said George, thinking, 'but as there's no bucket or anything, we can't get any. I was taking a big tin of fresh water with me – but we'd better fill two or three more tins now you are all coming! I know where there are some, quite clean and new.'

So they filled some tins with fresh water, and put them with the sacks, ready to take to the boat. It was so exciting doing all these things in the middle of the night! Anne could hardly keep her voice down to a whisper, and it was a wonder that Timothy didn't bark, for he sensed the excitement of the others.

There was a tin of cakes in the larder, freshly made, so those were added to the heap that was forming in the front garden. There was a large joint of meat too, and George wrapped it in a cloth and put that with the heap, telling Timmy in a fierce voice that if he so much as sniffed at it she would leave him behind!

'I've got my little stove for boiling water on, or heating

up anything,' whispered George. 'It's in the boat. That's what I bought the methylated spirit for, of course. You didn't guess, did you? And the matches for lighting it. I say – what about candles? We can't use our torches all the time, the batteries would soon run out.'

They found a pound of candles in the kitchen cupboard, a kettle, a saucepan, some old knives and forks and spoons, and a good many other things they thought they might possibly want. They also came across some small bottles of ginger-beer, evidently stored for their own use by the Sticks.

'All bought out of my mother's money!' said George. 'Well, we'll take the ginger-beer too. It will be nice to drink it on a hot day.'

'Where are we going to sleep at night?' said Julian. 'In that ruined part of the old castle, where there is just one room with a roof left, and walls?'

'That's where I planned to sleep,' said George. 'I was going to make my bed of some of the heather that grows on the island, covered by a rug or two, which I've got down in the boat.'

'We'll take all the rugs we can find,' said Julian. 'And some cushions for pillows. I say, isn't this simply thrilling? I don't know when I've felt so excited. I feel like a prisoner escaping to freedom! Won't the Sticks be amazed when they find us gone!'

'Yes – we'll have to decide what to say to them,' said George, rather soberly. 'We don't want them sending people after us to the island, making us come back. I don't think they should know we've gone there.'

'We'll discuss that later,' said Dick. 'The thing is to get

everything to the boat whilst it's dark. It will soon be dawn.'

'How are we going to get all this down to George's boat?' said Anne, looking at the enormous pile of goods by the light of her torch. 'We'll never be able to carry them all!'

Certainly it looked a great pile. Julian had an idea, as usual. 'Are there any barrows in the shed?' he asked George. 'If we could pile the things into a couple of barrows, we could easily take everything in one journey. We could wheel the barrows along on the sandy side of the road so that we don't make any noise.'

'Oh, good idea!' said George, delighted. 'I wish I'd thought of that before. I had to make about five journeys to and from the boat when I took my own things. There are two barrows in the shed. We'll get them. One has a squeaky wheel, but we'll hope no one hears it.'

Stinker heard the squeak, as he lay in a corner of Mrs. Stick's room. He pricked up his ears and growled softly. He did not dare to bark, for he was afraid of bringing Timothy up. Mrs. Stick did not hear the growl. She slept soundly, not even stirring. She had no idea what was going on downstairs.

The things were all stowed into the boat. The children didn't like leaving them there unguarded. In the end they decided to leave Dick there, sleeping on the rugs. They stood thinking for a moment before they went back without Dick.

'I do hope we've remembered all we shall want,' said George, wrinkling up her forehead. 'Golly – I know! We haven't remembered a tin-opener – nor a thing to take off the tops of the ginger-beer bottles. They've got those little tin lids that have to be forced off by an opener.'

'We'll put those in our pockets when we get back to the house and find them,' said Julian. 'I remember seeing some in the sideboard drawer. Good-bye, Dick. We'll be down very early to row off. We must get some bread at the baker's as soon as he opens, because we've got hardly any, and we'll see if we can pick up a very large bone at the butcher's for Timmy. George has got a bag of biscuits in the boat for him too.'

The three of them set off back to the house with Timmy, leaving Dick curled up comfortably on the rugs. He soon fell asleep again, his face upturned to the stars that would soon fade from the sky.

The others talked about what to tell the Sticks. 'I think we won't tell them anything,' said Julian, at last. 'I don't particularly want to tell them deliberate lies, and I'm certainly not going to tell them the truth. I know what we'll do — there is a train that leaves the station about eight o'clock, which would be the one we'd catch if we were going back to our own home. We'll find a time-table, leave it open on the dining-room table, as if we'd been looking up a train, and then we'll all set off across the moor at the back of the house, as if we were going to the station.'

'Oh yes — then the Sticks will think we've run away, and gone to catch the train back home,' said Anne. 'They will never guess we've gone to the island.'

'That's a good idea,' said George, pleased. 'But how shall we know when Father and Mother get back?'

'Is there anyone you could leave a message with — somebody you could really trust?' asked Julian.

George thought hard. 'There's Alf the fisher boy,' she said at last. 'He used to look after Tim for me when I wasn't allowed to have him in the house. I know he'd not give us away.'

'We'll call on Alf before we go then,' said Julian. 'Now, let's look for that time-table and lay it open on the table at the right place.'

They hunted for the time-table, found the right page, and underlined the train they hoped that the Sticks would think they were catching. They found the tin and bottle openers and put them into their pockets. Julian found two or three more boxes of matches too. He thought two would not last long enough.

By this time dawn had come and the house was being flooded with early sunshine. 'I wonder if the baker is open,' said Julian. 'We might as well go and see. It's about six o'clock.'

They went to the baker. He was not open, but the new loaves had already been made. The baker was outside, sunning himself. He had baked his bread at night, ready to sell it new-made in the morning. He grinned at the children.

'Up early today,' he said. 'What, you want some of my loaves – how many? Six! Good gracious, whatever for?'

'To eat,' said George, grinning. Julian paid for six enormous loaves, and they went to the butcher's. His shop was not open either, but the butcher himself was sweeping the path outside. 'Could we buy a very big bone for Timmy, please?' asked George. She got an enormous one, and Timmy looked at it longingly. Such a bone would last him for days, he knew!

'Now,' said Julian, as they set off to the boat, 'we'll pack
these things into the boat, then go back to the house, and
make a noise so that the Sticks know we're there. Then
we'll set off across the moors, and hope the Sticks will
think we are making for the train.'

They woke Dick, who was still sleeping peacefully in
the boat, and packed in the bread and bone.

'Take the boat into the next cove,' said George. 'Can
you do that? We shall be hidden there from anyone on
the beach then. The fishermen are all out in their boats,
fishing. We shan't be seen, if we set off in about an hour's
time. We'll be back by then.'

They went back to the house and made a noise as if
they were just getting up. George whistled to Timmy,
and Julian sang at the top of his voice. Then, with a great
banging of doors they set out down the path and cut
across the moors, in full sight of the kitchen window.

'Hope the Sticks won't notice Dick isn't with us,' said
Julian, seeing Edgar staring out of the window. 'I expect
they'll think he's gone ahead.'

They kept to the path until they came to a dip, where
they were hidden from any watcher at Kirrin Cottage.
Then they took another path that led them, unseen, to the
cove where Dick had taken the boat. He was there, waiting anxiously for them.

'Ahoy there!' yelled Julian, in excitement. 'The adventure is about to begin.'

Chapter Ten

KIRRIN ISLAND ONCE MORE!

THEY all clambered into the boat. Timothy leapt in lightly and ran to the prow, where he always stood. His tongue hung out in excitement. He knew quite well that something was up – and he was in it! No wonder he panted and wagged his tail hard.

'Off we go!' said Julian, taking the oars. 'Sit over there a bit, Anne. The luggage is weighing down the boat awfully the other end. Dick, sit by Anne to keep the balance better. That's right. Off we go!'

And off they went in George's boat, rocking up and down on the waves. The sea was fairly calm, but a good breeze blew through their hair. The water splashed round the boat and made a nice gurgly, friendly noise. The children all felt very happy. They were on their own. They were escaping from the horrid Sticks. They were going to stay on Kirrin Island, with the rabbits and gulls and jackdaws.

'Doesn't that new-made bread smell awfully good?' said Dick, feeling very hungry as usual. 'Can we just grab a bit, do you think?'

'Yes, let's,' said George. So they broke off bits of the warm brown crust, handed some to Julian, who was rowing, and chewed the delicious new-made bread. Timmy got a bit too, but his was gone as soon as it went into his mouth.

'Timmy's funny,' said Anne. 'He never eats his food as we do – he seems to *drink* it – just takes it into his mouth and swallows it, as if it was water!'

The others laughed. 'He doesn't drink his bones,' said George. 'He always eats those all right – chews on them for hours and hours. Don't you, Timothy?'

'Woof!' said Timmy, agreeing. He eyed the place where that enormous bone was, wishing he could have it now. But the children wouldn't let him. They were afraid it might go overboard, and that would be a pity.

'I don't believe anyone has noticed us going,' said Julian. 'Except Alf the fisher-boy, of course. We told him about going to the island, Dick, but nobody else.'

They had called at Alf's house on their way to the cove. Alf was alone in the yard at the back. His mother was away and his father was out fishing. They had told him their secret, and Alf had nodded his tousled head and promised faithfully to tell nobody at all. He was evidently very proud at being trusted.

'If my mother and father come back, you must let us know,' said George. 'Sail as near the island as you dare, and hail us. You can get nearer to it than anyone else.'

'I'll do that,' promised Alf, wishing he could go with them.

'So, you see, Dick,' said Julian, as he rowed out to the island, 'if by any chance Aunt Fanny does return sooner than we expect, we shall know at once and come back. I think we've planned everything very well.'

'Yes, we have,' said Dick. He turned and faced the island, which was coming nearer. 'We shall soon be there. Isn't George going to take the oars and guide the boat in?'

'Yes,' said George. 'We've come to the difficult bit now, where we've got to weave our way in and out of the different rocks that keep sticking up. Give me the oars, Ju.'

She took the oars, and the others watched in admiration as the girl guided the big boat skilfully in and out of the hidden rocks. She certainly was very clever. They felt perfectly safe with her.

The boat slid into the little cove. It was a natural harbour, with the water running up to a stretch of sand. High rocks sheltered it. The children jumped out eagerly, and four pairs of willing hands tugged the boat quickly up the sand.

'Higher up still,' panted George. 'You know what awful storms suddenly blow up in this bay. We want to be sure the boat is quite safe, no matter how high the seas run.'

The boat soon lay on one side, high up the stretch of sand. The children sat down, puffing and blowing. 'Let's have breakfast here,' said Julian. 'I don't feel like unloading all those heavy things at the moment. We'll get what we want for breakfast, and have it here on this warm bit of sand.'

They got a loaf of new bread, some cold ham, a few tomatoes and a pot of jam. Anne found knives and forks and plates. Julian opened two bottles of ginger-beer.

'Funny sort of breakfast,' he said, setting the bottles down on the sand, 'But simply gorgeous when anyone is as hungry as we are.'

They ate everything except about a third of the loaf. Timmy was given his bone and some of his own biscuits. He crunched up the biscuits at once, and then sat down contentedly to gnaw the fine bone.

'How nice to be Timmy – with no plate or knife or fork or cup to bother about,' said Anne, lying on her back in the sun, feeling that she really couldn't eat anything more. 'Oh, if we are always going to have mixed-up meals like this on the island, I shall never want to go back. Who would have thought that ham and jam and ginger-beer would go so well together?'

Timmy was thirsty. He sat with his tongue hanging out

wishing that George would give him a drink. He didn't
like ginger-beer.

George eyed him lazily.

'Oh Timmy – are you thirsty?' she said. 'Oh dear, I feel
as if I really can't get up! You'll have to wait a few
minutes, then I'll go to the boat and empty out some water
for you.'

But Timothy couldn't wait. He went off to some nearby
rocks, which were out of reach of the sea. In a hole in one
of them he found some rain-water, and he lapped it up
eagerly. The children heard him lapping it, and laughed.

'Isn't Timmy clever?' murmured Anne. 'I should never
have thought of that.'

The children had been up half the night, and now
they were full of good things, and were very sleepy. One
by one they fell asleep on the warm sand. Timothy eyed
them in astonishment. It wasn't night-time! Yet here
were all the children sleeping tightly. Well, well – a dog
could always go to sleep too at any time! So Timothy
threw himself down beside George, put his head right on
her middle, and closed his eyes.

The sun was high when the little company awoke.
Julian awoke first, then Dick, feeling very hot indeed, for
the sun was blazing down. They sat up, yawning.

'Goodness!' said Dick, looking at his arms. 'The sun
has caught me properly. I shall be terribly sore by tonight.
Did we bring any cream, Julian?'

'No. We never thought of it,' said Julian. 'Cheer up!
You'll be burnt much more by the time this day ends.
The sun's going to be awfully hot – there's not a cloud in
the sky!'

They woke up the girls. George pushed Timmy's head
off her tummy. 'You give me nightmares when you put
your heavy head there,' she complained. 'Oh, I say –
we're on the island, aren't we? For a moment I thought I
was back in bed at Kirrin Cottage!'

'Isn't it gorgeous – here we are for ages, all by ourselves,
with tons of nice things to eat, able to do just what we
like!' said Anne, contentedly.

'I guess the old Sticks are glad we've gone,' said Dick.
'Spotty Face will be able to loll in the sitting-room and
read all our books, if he wants to.'

'And Stinker-dog will be able to wander all over the
house and lie on anybody's bed without being afraid
that Timothy will eat him whole,' said George. 'Well, let
him. I don't care about anything now that I've escaped.'

It was fun to lie there and talk about everything. But
soon Julian, who could never rest for long, once he was
awake, got up and stretched himself.

'Come on!' he said to the others. 'There is work to do,
Lazy-Bones! Come along!'

'Work to do? What do you mean?' said George in
astonishment.

'Well, we've got to unload the boat and pack everything somewhere where it won't get spoilt if the rain happens to come,' said Julian. 'And we've got to decide
exactly where we're going to sleep, and get the heather
for our beds and pile the rugs on them. There's plenty to
do!'

'Oh, don't let's do it yet,' said Anne, not at all wanting
to get up out of the warm sand. But the others pulled her
up, and together they all set to work to unload the boat.

'Let's go and have a look at the castle,' said Julian. And find the little room where we'll sleep. It's the only one left whole, so it will have to be that one.'

They went right to the top of the inlet, climbed up on to the rocks and made their way towards the old ruined castle, whose walls rose up from the middle of the little island. They stopped to gaze at it.

'It's a fine old ruin,' said Dick. 'Aren't we lucky to have an island and a castle of our own! Fancy, this is all ours!'

They gazed through a big broken-down archway, to old steps beyond. The castle had once had two fine towers, but now one was almost gone. The other rose high in the air, half-ruined. The black jackdaws collected there, talking loudly. 'Chack, chack, chack! Chack, chack, chack!'

'Nice birds,' said Dick. 'I like them. See the grey patch at the back of their heads, Anne? I wonder if they ever stop talking.'

'I don't think so,' said George. 'Oh, look at the rabbits – tamer than ever!'

The courtyard was full of big rabbits, who eyed them as they came near. It really seemed as if it would be possible to pat them, they were so tame – but one by one they edged away as the children approached.

Timothy was in a great state of excitement, and his tail quivered from end to end. Oh those rabbits! Why couldn't he chase them? Why was George so difficult about rabbits? Why couldn't he make them run a bit?

But George had her hand on his collar, and gave him a stern glance. 'Now, Timothy, don't you *dare* to chase even the smallest of these rabbits. They're mine, every one of them.'

'Ours!' corrected Anne at once. She wanted to share in the rabbits, as well as in the castle and the island.

'Ours!' said George. 'Let's go and have a look at the little dark room where we'll spend the nights.'

They made their way to where the castle did not seem to be quite so ruined. They came to a doorway and looked inside.

'Here it is!' said Julian, peeping in. 'I shall have to use my torch. The windows are only slits here, and it's quite dark.'

He turned on his torch – and the children all gazed into the old room where they proposed to store their goods and sleep.

George gave a loud exclamation. 'Golly! We can't use this room! The roof has fallen in since last summer.'

So it had. Julian's torch shone on to a heap of fallen stones, scattered all over the floor. It was quite impossible to use the old room now. In any case it might be dangerous to do so, for it looked as if more stones might fall at any moment.

'Blow!' said Julian. 'What shall we do about this? We shall have to find somewhere else for a storing and sleeping-place!'

Chapter Eleven

ON THE OLD WRECK

IT was quite a shock to have their plans spoilt. They knew there was no other room in the ruined castle that was sufficiently whole to shelter them. And they must find some sort of shelter, for although the weather was fine at the moment, it might rain hard any day – or a storm might blow up.

'And storms round about Kirrin are so very violent,' said Julian, remembering one or two. 'Do you remember the storm that tossed your wreck up from the bottom of the sea, George?'

'Oh yes,' said George and Anne, together, and Anne added eagerly: 'Let's go and see the wreck today if we can. I'd love to see if it's still balanced on those rocks, as it was last year, when we explored it.'

'Well, first we must make up our minds where we are going to sleep,' said Julian, firmly. 'I don't know if you realize it, but it's about three o'clock in the afternoon! We slept for hours on the sand – tired out with our exciting night, I suppose. We really must find some safe place and put our things there at once, and make beds.'

'Well, but where shall we go?' said Dick. 'There's no other place in the old castle.'

'There's the dungeon below,' said Anne, shivering. 'But I don't want to go there. It's so dark and mysterious.'

Nobody wanted to sleep down in the dungeons! Dick

frowned and thought hard. 'What about the wreck?' F
said. 'Any chance of living there?'

'We might go and see,' said Julian. 'I don't someho
fancy living on a damp old rotting wreck – but if it's sti
high on the rocks, maybe the sun will have dried it, an
it might be possible to have our bed and stores there.'

'Let's go and see now,' said George. So they made the
way from the ruined castle to the old wall that ran roun
it. From there they would be able to see the wreck. It ha
been cast up the year before, and had settled firmly o
some rocks.

They stood on the wall and looked for the wreck, b
it was not where they had expected it. 'It's moved,' sai
Julian, in surprise. 'There it is, look, on those rocks
nearer to the shore than it was before. Poor old wreck
It's been battered about a good bit this last winter, hasn
it? It looks much more of a real wreck than it did la
summer.'

'I don't believe we shall be able to sleep there,' sai
Dick. 'It's dreadfully battered. We might be able to sto
food there, though. Do you know, I believe we could g
to it from those rocks that run out from the island.'

'Yes, I believe we could,' said George. 'We could on
reach it safely by boat last summer – but when the tide
down, I think we *could* climb out over the line of rock
right to the wreck itself.'

'We'll try in about an hour,' said Julian, feeling e:
cited. 'The tide will be off the rocks by then.'

'Let's go and have a look at the old well,' said Dic
and they made their way back to the courtyard of th
castle. Here, the summer before, they had found th

ntrance to the well-shaft that ran deep down through
he rock, past the dungeons below, lower than the level of
he sea, to fresh water.

The children looked about for the well, and came to
he old wooden cover. They drew it back.

'There are the rungs of the old iron ladder I went
own last year,' said Dick, peering in. 'Now let's find the
ntrance to the dungeon. The steps down into it are somewhere near here.'

They found the entrance, but to their surprise some
normous stones had been pulled across it. 'Who did

that?' said George, frowning. 'We didn't! Someone ha
been here!'

'Trippers, I suppose,' said Julian. 'Do you remembe
that we thought we saw a spire of smoke here the othe
day? I bet it was trippers. You know, the story of Kirri
Island, and its old castle and dungeons, and the treasur
we found in it last year, was all in the newspapers. I ex
pect one of the fishermen has been making money by tak
ing trippers and landing them on *our* island.'

'How dare they?' said George, looking very fierce. '
shall put up a board that says "Trespassers will be ser
to prison." I won't have strangers on our island.'

'Well, don't worry about the stones pulled across th
dungeon entrance,' said Julian. 'I don't think any of u
want to go down there. Look at poor old Timmy! He'
gazing at those rabbits most unhappily. Isn't he funny

Timothy was sitting down behind the children, lookin
most mournfully at the ring of rabbits all round the weed
grown courtyard. He looked at the rabbits and then h
looked at George, then he looked back at the rabbits.

'No good, Timmy,' said George, firmly. 'I'm not goin;
to change my mind about rabbits. You're not to chas
them on our island.'

'I expect he thinks you're most unfair to him,' sai
Anne. 'After all, you said he might share your quarter o
the island with you – and so he thinks he ought to hav
his share of your rabbits too!'

Everyone laughed. Timmy wagged his tail and looke
hopefully at George. They all walked across the court
yard – and then Julian suddenly came to a stop.

'Look!' he said in surprise, pointing to something o

the ground. 'Look! Someone *has* been here! This is where they built a fire!'

Everyone gazed at the ground. There was a heap of wood-ash there, quite evidently left from a fire. Stamped into the ground was a cigarette end, too. There was absolutely no doubt about it – someone had been on the island!

'If trippers come here I'll set Timmy on to them!' cried George, in a fury. 'This is our own place, it doesn't belong to anybody else at all. Timothy, you mustn't chase rabbits here, but you can chase anybody on two legs, except us! See?

Timmy wagged his tail at once. 'Woof!' he said, quite agreeing. He looked all round as if he hoped to see somebody appearing that he could chase. But there was no one.

'I should think the tide is about off those rocks by now,' said Julian. 'Let's go and see. If it is we'll climb along them and see if we can get to the wreck. Anne had better not come. She might slip and fall, and the sea is raging all round the rocks.'

'Of course I'm coming!' cried Anne, indignantly. 'You're just as likely to fall as I am.'

'Well, I'll see if it looks too dangerous,' said Julian. They made their way over the castle wall, down to the line of rocks that ran out seawards, towards the wreck. Big waves did wash over the rocks occasionally, but it seemed fairly safe.

'If you keep between me and Dick, you can come, Anne,' said Julian. 'But you must let us help you over difficult parts, and not make a fuss. We don't want you to fall in and get washed away.'

They began to make their way along the line of rugged
slippery rocks. The tide went down even farther as they
got nearer to the wreck, and soon there was very little
danger of being washed off the rocks. It was possible now
to get right to the wreck across the rocks – a thing they
had not been able to do the summer before.

'Here we are!' said Julian at last, and he put his hand
on the side of the old wreck. She was a big ship now that
they were near to her. She towered above them, thick
with shell-fish and seaweed, smelling musty and old. The
water washed round the bottom part of her, but the top
part was right out of the water, even when the tide was
at its highest.

'She's been thrown about a bit last winter,' said George,
looking at her. 'There are a lot more new holes in her
side, aren't there? And part of her old mast is gone, and
some of the deck. How can we get up to her.'

'I've got a rope,' said Julian, and he undid a rope that
he had wound round his waist. 'Half a minute – I'll make
a loop and see if I can throw it round that post sticking out
up there.'

He threw the rope two or three times, but could not
get the loop round the post. George took it from him impatiently. At the first throw she got it round the post. She
was very good indeed at things like that – better than a
boy in some things, Anne thought admiringly.

She was up the rope like a monkey, and soon stood on
the sloping slippery deck. She almost slipped, but caught
at a broken piece of deck just in time. Julian helped Anne
to go up, and then the two boys followed.

'It's a horrid smell, isn't it?' said Anne, wrinkling up

er nose. 'Do all wrecks smell like this? I don't think I'll
o and look down in the cabins like we did last time. The
nell would be worse there.'

So the others left Anne up on the half-rotten deck
rhilst they went to explore a bit. They went down to the
nelly, seaweed-hung cabins, and into the captain's old
abin, the biggest of the lot. But it was quite plain that
ot only could they not sleep there, but they could
ertainly not hope to store anything there, either. The
rhole place was damp and rotten. Julian was half afraid
is foot would go through the planking at any moment.

'Let's go up to the deck,' he said. 'It's nasty down
ere – awfully dark too.'

They were just going up, when they heard a shout from
nne. 'I say! Come here, quick! I've found something!'

They hurried up as fast as they could, slipping and
iding on the sloping deck. Anne was standing where
ey had left her, her eyes shining brightly. She was point-
ig to something on the opposite side of the ship.

'What is it?' said George. 'What's the matter?'

'Look – that wasn't here when we came here before,
irely!' said Anne, still pointing. The others looked where
ie pointed. They saw an open locker at the other side
f the deck, and stuffed into it was a small black trunk!
ow extraordinary!

'A little black trunk!' said Julian, in surprise. 'No –
iat wasn't there before. It's not been there long either –
's quite dry and new! Whoever does it belong to? And
hy should it be here?'

Chapter Twelve

THE CAVE IN THE CLIFF

CAUTIOUSLY the children made their way down the slippery deck towards the locker. The door of this had evidently been shut on the trunk, but had come open, so that the trunk was not hidden, as had been intended.

Julian pulled out the little black trunk. All the children were amazed. *Why* should anyone put a trunk there?

'Smugglers, do you think?' said Dick, his eyes gleaming.

'Yes – it might be,' said Julian, thoughtfully, trying to undo the straps of the trunk. 'This would be a very good place for smugglers. Ships that knew the way could put in cast off a boat with smuggled goods, leave them here, and go on their way, knowing that people could come and collect the goods at their leisure.'

'Do you think there are smuggled goods inside the trunk?' asked Anne, in excitement. 'What would there be? Diamonds? Silks?'

'Anything that has a duty to be paid on it before it can get into the country,' said Julian. 'Blow these straps I can't undo them.'

'Let *me* try,' said Anne, who had very deft little fingers. She began to work at the buckles, and in a short time had the straps undone. But a further disappointment awaited them. The trunk was well and truly locked! There were two good locks, and no keys!

'Blow!' said George. 'How sickening! How can we get the trunk open now?'

'We can't,' said Julian. 'And we mustn't smash it open, because it would warn whoever it belongs to that the goods had been found. We don't want to warn the smugglers that we have discovered their little game. We want to try and catch them!'

'Ooooh!' said Anne, going red with excitement. 'Catch it's absolutely *full* of them. This will be the third one we could?'

'Why not?' said Julian. 'No one knows we are here. If we hid whenever we saw a ship approaching the island, we might see a boat coming to it, and we could watch and find out what is happening. I should think that the smugglers are using this island as a sort of dropping-place for goods. I wonder who comes and fetches them? Someone from Kirrin Village or the nearby places, I should think.'

'This is going to be awfully exciting,' said Dick. 'We always seem to have adventures when we come to Kirrin. It's absolutely *full* of them. This will be the third one we have had.'

'I think we ought to be getting back over the rocks,' said Julian, suddenly looking over the side of the ship and seeing that the tide had turned. 'Come on – we don't want to be caught by the tide and have to stay here for hours and hours! I'll go down the rope first. Then you come, Anne.'

They were soon climbing over the rocks again, feeling very excited. Just as they reached the last stretch of rocks leading to the rocky cliff of the island itself, Dick topped.

'What's up?' said George, pushing behind him. 'Do get on!'

'Isn't that a cave, just beyond that big rock there?' said Dick, pointing. 'It looks awfully like one to me. If it was, it would be a simply lovely place to store our things in, and even to sleep in, if it was out of reach of the sea.'

'There aren't any caves on Kirrin,' began George, and then she stopped short. What Dick was pointing at really did look like a cave. It was worth while seeing if it was one. After all, George had never explored this line of rocks, and so had never been able to catch sight of the cave that lay just beyond. It could not possibly be seen from the land.

'We'll go and see,' she said. So they changed their direction, and instead of climbing back the way they had come, they cut across the mass of rock and made their way towards a jutting-out part of the cliff, in which the cave seemed to be.

They came to it at last. Steep rocks guarded the entrance, and half hid it. Except from where Dick had seen it, it was really impossible to catch sight of it, it was so well-hidden.

'It *is* a cave!' said Dick, in delight, stepping into it. 'And my, what a fine one!'

It really was a beauty. Its floor was spread with fine white sand, as soft as powder, and perfectly dry, for the cave was clearly higher than the tide reached, except, possibly in a bad winter storm. Round one side of it ran a stone ledge.

'Exactly like a shelf made for us!' cried Anne, in joy. 'We can put all our things here. How lovely! Let's come and live here and sleep here. And look, Julian – we've even got a skylight in the roof!'

The little girl pointed upwards, and the others saw that the roof of the cave was open in one part, giving on to the cliff-top itself. It was plain that somewhere on the leathery cliff above was a hole that looked down to the cave, making what Anne called a 'skylight'.

'We could drop all our things down through that hole,' said Julian, quickly making plans. 'We would have an awful time bringing them over the rocks. If we can find that hole up there when we are out on the cliff again, we can let down everything on a rope. It's not a very high "skylight", as Anne calls it, for the cliffs are low just here. I believe we could swing ourselves down a rope easily, so that we needn't have the bother of clambering over the rocks to the seaward entrance we have just come in by!'

This was a grand discovery. 'Our island is even more exciting than we thought,' said Anne, happily. 'We've got a beautiful cave to share now!'

The next thing to do, of course, was to go up on the cliff and find the hole that led to the roof of the cave. So out they all went, Timmy too. Timmy was funny on the slippery rocks. His feet slithered about, and two or three times he fell into the water. But he just swam across the pools he fell into, clambered out and went on again with his slithering.

'He's like George!' said Anne, with a laugh. 'He never gives up, whatever happens to him!'

They climbed up to the top of the cliff. It was easy to find the hole once they knew it was there.

'Pretty dangerous, really,' said Julian, when he had

found it, and was peering down. 'Any one of us might have run on this cliff and popped down the hole by accident. See, it's all criss-crossed with blackberry brambles.

They scratched their hands, trying to free the hole from the brambles. Once they had cleared the hole, they could look right down into the cave quite easily.

'It's not very far down,' said Anne. 'It looks almost as if we could jump down, if we let ourselves slide down this hole.'

'Don't you do anything of the sort,' said Julian. 'You'd break your leg. Wait till we get a rope fixed up, hanging down into the cave. Then we can manage to get in and out easily.'

They went back to the boat, and began unloading it. They took everything across to the seaward side of the island, where the cave was. Julian took a strong rope and knotted it thickly at intervals.

'To give our feet a hold as we go down,' he explained. 'If we drop down too quickly, we'll hurt our hands. These knots will stop us dropping down and help us to climb up.'

'Let me go down first, and then you can lower all our things to me,' said George. So down she went, hand over hand, her feet easily finding the thick knots, feeling for one after another. It was a good way to go down.

'How shall we get Timmy down?' said Julian. But Timothy, who had been whining anxiously at the edge of the hole, watching George sliding away from him, solved the difficulty himself.

He jumped into the hole and disappeared down it! There came a shriek from below.

'Oh! My goodness, what's this! Oh *Timmy*! Have you hurt yourself?'

The sand was very soft, like a velvet cushion and Tim had not hurt himself at all. He gave himself a shake and then barked joyfully. He was with George again! He wasn't going to have his mistress disappearing down mysterious holes without following her at once. Not Timmy!

Then followed the business of lowering down all the goods. Anne and Dick tied the things together in rugs, and Julian lowered them carefully. George untied the rope as soon as it reached her, took out the goods, and then back went the rope again to be tied round another bundle.

'Last one!' called Julian, after a long spell of really hard work. 'Then down we come too. and I don't mind telling you that before we make our beds or anything, our next job is to have a jolly good meal! It's hours and hours since we had a meal, and I'm starving.'

Soon they were all sitting on the warm soft floor of the cave. They opened a tin of meat, cut huge slices of bread and made sandwiches, Then they opened a tin of pine-apple chunks and ate those, spooning them out of the tin, full of sweetness and juice. After that they still felt hungry, so they opened two tins of sardines and dug them out with biscuits. It made a really grand meal.

'Ginger-pop to finish up with please,' said Dick. 'My word, why don't people always have meals like this?'

'We'd better hurry up or we shan't be able to get heather for our beds,' said George, sleepily.

'Who wants heather?' said Dick. '*I* don't! This lovely

soft sand is all *I* shall want – and a cushion and a rug o
two. I shall sleep better here than ever I did in bed!'

So the rugs and cushions were spread out on the sand
floor of the cave. A candle was lighted as it grew dark
and the four sleepy children looked at one another
Timmy, as usual, was with George.

'Good night,' said George. 'I can't keep awake an
other minute. 'Good night, ev ... ery ... body ... good
... night!'

Chapter Thirteen

A DAY ON THE ISLAND

THE children hardly knew where they were the next day when they woke up. The sun was pouring into the cave entrance, and fell first of all on George's sleeping face. It awoke her and she lay half-dozing, wondering why her bed felt rather less soft than usual.

'But I'm not in my bed – I'm on Kirrin Island, of course!' she thought suddenly to herself. She sat up and gave Anne a punch. 'Wake up, sleepy-head! We're on the island!'

Soon they were all awake rubbing the sleep from their eyes. 'I think I'm going to get heather today for my bed, after all,' said Anne. 'The sand feels soft at first, but it gets hard after a bit.'

The others agreed that they would all get heather for their beds, set on the sand, with rugs for covering. Then they would have really fine beds.

'It's fun to live in a cave,' said Dick. 'Fancy having a fine cave like this on our island, as well as a castle and dungeons! We are really very lucky.'

'I feel sticky and dirty,' said Julian. 'Let's go and have a bathe before we have breakfast. Then cold ham, bread, pickles and marmalade for me!'

'We shall be cold after our bathe,' said George. 'We'd better light my little stove and put the kettle on to boil whilst we're bathing. Then we can make some hot cocoa when we come back shivering!'

'Oh yes,' said Anne, who had never boiled anything on such a tiny stove before. 'Do let's. I'll fill the kettle with water from one of the tins. What shall we do for milk?'

'There's a tin of milk somewhere in the pile,' said Julian. 'We can open that. Where's the tin-opener?'

It was not to be found which was most exasperating. But at last Julian discovered it in his shorts pocket, so all was well.

The little stove was filled with methylated spirit, and lighted. The kettle was filled and set on top. Then the children went off to bathe.

'Look! There's a simply marvellous pool in the middle of those rocks over there!' called Julian, pointing. 'We've never spotted it before. Golly, it's like a small swimming-pool, made specially for us!'

'Kirrin Swimming Pool, a shilling a dip!' said Dick. 'Free to the owners, though! Come on – it looks gorgeous! And see how the waves keep washing over the top of the rocks and splashing into the pool. Couldn't be better!'

It really was a lovely rock-pool, deep, clear and not too cold. The children enjoyed themselves thoroughly, splashing about and swimming and floating. George tried a dive off one of the rocks, and went in beautifully.

'George can do anything in the water,' said Anne, admiringly. 'I wish I could dive and swim like George. But I never shall.'

'We can see the old wreck nicely from here,' said Julian, coming out of the water. 'Blow! We didn't bring any towels.'

'We'll use one of the rugs, turn and turn about,' said

Dick. 'I'll go and fetch the thinnest one. I say – do you remember that trunk we saw in the wreck yesterday? Odd, wasn't it?'

'Yes, very odd,' said Julian. 'I don't understand it. We'll have to keep a watch on the wreck and see who comes to collect the trunk.'

'I suppose the smugglers – if they are smugglers – will come slinking round this side of the island and quietly send off a boat to the wreck,' said George, drying herself vigorously. 'Well, we'd better keep a strict look-out, and see if anything appears on the sea out there in the way of a small steamer, boat or ship.'

'Yes. We don't want them to spot us,' said Dick. 'We shan't find out anything if they see us and are warned. They'd at once give up coming to the island. I vote we each of us take turns at keeping a look-out, so that we can spot anything at once and get under cover.'

'Good idea!' said Julian. 'Well, I'm dry, but not very warm. Let's race to the cave, and get that hot drink. And breakfast – golly, I could eat a whole chicken and probably a duck as well, to say nothing of a turkey.'

The others laughed. They all felt the same. They raced off to the cave, running over the sand and climbing over a few rocks, then down to the cave-beach and into the big entrance, still splashed with sunshine.

The kettle was boiling away merrily, sending a cloud of steam up from its tin spout. 'Get the ham out and a loaf of bread, and that jar of pickles we brought,' ordered Julian. 'I'll open the tin of milk. George, you take the tin of cocoa and that jug, and make enough for all of us.'

'I'm so terribly happy,' said Anne, as she sat at the entrance to the cave, eating her breakfast. 'It's a lovely feeling. It's simply gorgeous being on our island like this all by ourselves, able to do what we like.'

They all felt the same. It was such a lovely day too and the sky and sea were so blue. They sat eating and drinking, gazing out to sea, watching the waves break into spray over the rocks beyond the old wreck. It certainly was a very rocky coast.

'Let's arrange everything very nicely in the cave,' said Anne, who was the tidiest of the four, and always liked to play at 'houses' if she could. 'This shall be our house our home. We'll make four proper beds. And we'll each have our own place to sit in. And we'll arrange everything tidily on that big stone shelf there. It might have been made for us!'

'We'll leave Anne to play "houses" by herself,' said George, who was longing to stretch her legs again. 'We'll go and get some heather for beds. And oh! – what about one of us keeping a watch on the old wreck, to see who comes there?'

'Yes – that's important,' said Julian at once. 'I'll take first watch. The best place would be up on the cliff just above this cave. I can find a gorse bush that will hide me all right from anyone out at sea. You others get the heather. We will take two-hourly watches. We can read if we like, so long as we keep on looking up.'

Dick and George went to get the heather. Julian climbed up the knotted rope that still hung down through the hole, tied firmly to the great old root of an enormous

gorse bush. He pulled himself out on the cliff and lay on
the heather panting.

He could see nothing out to sea at all except for some
big steamer miles out on the sky-line. He lay down in the
sun, enjoying the warmth that poured into every inch of
his body. This look-out job was going to be very nice!

He could hear Anne singing down in the cave as she
tidied up her 'house'. Her voice came up through the
cave-roof hole, rather muffled. Julian smiled. He knew
Anne was enjoying herself thoroughly.

So she was. She had washed the few bits of crockery
they had used for breakfast, in a most convenient little
rain-pool outside the cave. Timmy used it for drinking-
water too, but he didn't seem to mind Anne using it for
washing-up water, though she apologized to him for
doing so.

'I'm sorry if I spoil your drinking water, Timmy darling,' she said, 'but you are such a sensible dog that I
know if it suddenly tastes nasty to you, you will go off
and find another rain pool.'

'Woof!' said Timmy, and ran off to meet George,
who was just arriving back with Dick, armed with masses
of soft, sweet-smelling heather for beds.

'Put the heather outside the cave, please George,' said
Anne. 'I'll make the beds inside when I'm ready.'

'Right!' said George. 'We'll go and get some more.
Aren't we having fun?'

'Julian's gone up the rope to the top of the cliff,' said
Anne. 'He'll yell if he sees anything unusual. I hope he
does, don't you?'

'It would be exciting,' agreed Dick, putting down his

heather on top of Timmy, and nearly burying him. 'Oh sorry Timmy – are you there? Bad luck!'

Anne had a very happy morning. She arranged everything beautifully on the shelf – crockery and knives and forks and spoons in one place – saucepan and kettle in another – tins of meat next, tins of soup together, tins of fruit neatly piled on top of one another. It really was a splendid larder and dresser!

She wrapped all the bread up in an old tablecloth they had brought, and put it at the back of the cave in the coolest place she could find. The tins of water went there too, and so did all the bottles of drinks.

Then the little girl set to work to make the beds. She

decided to make two nice big ones, one on each side of the cave.

'George and I and Tim will have the one this side,' she thought, busy patting down the heather into the shape of a bed. 'And Julian and Dick can have the other side. I shall want lots more heather. Oh, is that you, Dick? You're just in time! I want more heather.'

Soon the beds were made beautifully, and each had an old rug for an under-blanket, and two better rugs for covers. Cushions made pillows.

'What a pity we didn't bring night-things,' thought Anne. 'I could have folded them neatly and put them under the cushions. There! It all looks lovely. We've got a beautiful house.'

Julian came sliding down the rope from the cliff to the cave. He looked round admiringly. 'My word, Anne — the cave does look fine! Everything in order and looking so tidy. You are a good little girl.'

Anne was pleased to hear Julian's praise, though she didn't like him calling her a little girl.

'Yes, it does look nice, doesn't it?' she said. 'But why aren't you watching up on the cliff, Ju?'

'It's Dick's turn now,' said Julian. 'The two hours are up. Did we bring any biscuits? I feel as if I could do with one or two, and I bet the others could too. Let's all go up to the cliff-top and have some. George and Timmy are there with Dick.'

Anne knew exactly where to put her hand on the tin of biscuits. She took out ten and climbed up to the cliff-top. Julian went up on the rope. Soon all five were sitting by the big gorse-bush, nibbling at biscuits, Timmy too. At least, he didn't nibble. He just swallowed.

The day passed very pleasantly and rather lazily. They took turns at being look-out, though Anne was severely scolded by Julian in the afternoon for falling asleep during her watch. She was very ashamed of herself and cried.

'You're too little to be a look-out, that's what it is,' said Julian. 'We three and Timmy had better do it.'

'Oh, no, do let me too,' begged Poor Anne. 'I never never will fall asleep again. But the sun was so hot and . . .'

'Don't make excuses,' said Julian. 'It only makes things worse if you do. All right – we'll give you another chance Anne, and see if you are really big enough to do the things we do.'

But though they all took their turns, and kept a watch on the sea for any strange vessel, none appeared. The children were disappointed. They did so badly want to know who had put that trunk on the wreck and why, and what it contained.

'Better go to bed now,' said Julian, when the sun sank low. 'It's about nine o'clock. Come on! I'm really looking forward to a sleep on those lovely heathery beds that Anne has made so nicely!'

Chapter Fourteen

DISTURBANCE IN THE NIGHT

It was dark in the cave, not really quite dark enough to light a candle, but the cave looked so nice by candle-light that it was fun to light one. So Anne took down the candle-stick and lighted the candle. At once queer shadows jumped all round the cave, and it became a rather exciting place, not at all like the cave they knew by daylight!

'I wish we could have a fire,' said Anne.

'We'd be far too hot,' said Julian. 'And it would smoke us out. You can't have a fire in a cave like this. There's no chimney.'

'Yes, there is,' said Anne, pointing to the hole in the roof. 'If we lighted a fire just under that hole, it would act as a chimney, wouldn't it?'

'It might,' said Dick, thoughtfully. 'But I don't think so. We'd simply get the cave full of stifling smoke, and we wouldn't be able to sleep for choking.'

'Well, couldn't we light a fire at the cave entrance then?' said Anne who felt that a real home ought to have a fire somewhere. 'Just to keep away wild beasts, say! That's what the people of old times did. It says so in my history book. They lighted fires at the cave entrance at night to keep away any wild animal that might be prowl-ing around.'

'Well, what wild beasts do you think are likely to come

and peep into this cave?' asked Julian, lazily, finishing up a cup of cocoa. 'Lions? Tigers? Or perhaps you are afraid of an elephant or two.'

Everyone laughed. 'No – I don't really think animals like that would come,' said Anne. 'Only – it would be nice to have a red, glowing fire to watch when we go to sleep.'

'Perhaps Anne thinks the rabbits might come in and nibble our toes or something,' said Dick.

'Woof!' said Tim, pricking up his ears as he always did at the mention of rabbits.

'I don't think we ought to have a fire,' said Julian, 'because it might be seen out at sea and give a warning to anyone thinking of coming to the island to do a bit of smuggling.'

'Oh no, Julian – the entrance to this cave is so well-hidden that I'm sure no one could see a fire out to sea,' said George, at once. 'There's that line of high rocks in front, which must hide it completely. I think it would be rather fun to have a fire. It would light up the cave so queerly and excitingly.'

'Oh good, George!' said Anne, delighted to find someone agreeing with her.

'Well, we can't possibly fag out and get sticks for it now,' said Dick, who was far too comfortable to move.

'You don't need to,' said Anne, eagerly. 'I got plenty myself today, and stored them at the back of the cave, in case we wanted a fire.'

'Isn't she a good little house-wife!' said Julian, in great admiration. 'She may go to sleep when she's look-out, but she's wide-awake enough when it comes to

making a house for us out of a cave! All right, Anne –
we'll make a fire for you!'

They all got up and fetched the sticks from the back of
the cave. Anne had been to the jackdaw tower and had
picked up armfuls that the birds had dropped when making their nests in the tower. They built them up to make a
nice little fire. Julian got some dried seaweed too, to drop
into it.

They lighted the fire at the cave-entrance, and the
dry sticks blazed up at once. The children went back to
their heather-beds, and lay down on them, watching the
red flames leaping and crackling. The red glow lit up the
cave and made it very weird and exciting.

'This is lovely,' said Anne, half-asleep. 'Really lovely.
Oh Timmy, move a bit do. You're so heavy on my feet.
Here, George, pull Timothy over to your side. You're used
to him lying on you.'

'Good night,' said Dick, sleepily. 'The fire is dying
down, but I can't be bothered to put any more wood on it.
I'm sure all the lions and tigers and bears and elephants
have been frightened away.'

'Silly!' said Anne. 'You needn't tease me about it –
you've enjoyed it as much as I have! Good night.'

They all fell asleep and dreamed peacefully of many
things. Julian awoke with a jump. Some queer noise
had awakened him. He lay still, listening.

Timothy was growling deeply, right down in his throat.
'R-r-r-r-r-r-r,' he went. 'Gr-r-r-r-r-r-r-r!'

George awoke too, and put out her hand sleepily.
'What's the matter, Tim?' she said.

He's heard something, George,' said Julian, in a

ow voice from his bed on the other side of the cave.

George sat up cautiously. Timmy was still growling.
Sh!' said George and he stopped. He was sitting up
traight, his ears well cocked.

'Perhaps it's the smugglers come in the night,' whis-
ered George, and a funny prickly feeling ran down her
back. Somehow smugglers in the day time were rather
xciting and quite welcome – but at night they seemed
lifferent. George didn't at all want to meet any just
hen!

'I'm going out to see if I can spy anything,' said Julian,
etting off his bed quietly, so as not to wake Dick. 'I'll
o up the rope to the top of the cliff. I can see better from
here.'

'Take my torch,' said George. But Julian didn't want
t.

'No, thanks. I can feel the way up that knotted rope
uite well, whether I can see or not,' he said.

He went up the rope in the dark, his body twisting
ound as the rope turned. He climbed up on to the cliff
nd looked out to sea. It was a very dark night, and he
ould see no ship at all, not even the wreck. It was far too
lark.

'Pity there's no moon,' thought Julian. 'I might be
ble to see something then.'

He watched for a few minutes, and then George's voice
ame through the hole in the roof, coming out queerly at
is feet.

'Julian! Is there anything to see? Shall I come up?'

'Nothing at all,' said Julian. 'Is Timmy still growl-
ng?'

'Yes, when I take my hand off his collar,' said George
'I can't imagine what's upset him.'

Suddenly Julian caught sight of something. It was
light, a good way beyond the line of rocks. He watched
in excitement. That would be just about where the wreck
was! Yes – it must be someone on the wreck with a lantern!

'George! Come up!' he said, putting his head inside
the hole.

George came up, hand over hand, like a monkey, leaving Timothy growling below. She sat by Julian on the cliff-
top. 'See the wreck – look, over there!' said Julian. 'At
least, you can't see the wreck itself, it's too dark – but you
can see a lantern that someone has put there.'

'Yes – that's someone on our wreck, with a lantern,'
said George, feeling excited. 'Oh, I wonder if it's the
smugglers – coming to bring more things.'

'Or somebody fetching that trunk,' said Julian. 'Well,
we'll know tomorrow, for we'll go and see. Look! – whoever is there is moving off now – the light of the lantern's
going lower – they must be getting into a boat by the side
of the wreck. And now the light's gone out.'

The children strained their ears to hear if they could
discover the splash of oars or the sound of voices over the
water. They both thought they could hear voices.

'The boat must have gone off to join a ship or something,' said Julian. 'I believe I can see a faint light right
out there – out to sea, look! Maybe the boat is going to
it.'

There was nothing more to see or hear, and soon the
two of them slid down the knotted rope back to the cave

They didn't wake the others, who were still sleeping peacefully. Timothy leapt up and licked Julian and George,
whining joyfully. He did not growl any more.

'You're a good dog, aren't you?' said Julian, patting
him. 'Nothing ever escapes *your* sharp ears, does it?'

Timothy settled down on George's feet again. It was
plain that whatever it was that had disturbed him had
gone. It must have been the presence of the stranger or
strangers on the old wreck. Well, they would go there in
the morning and see if they could discover what had been
taken away or brought there in the night.

Anne and Dick were most indignant the next morning
when they heard Julian's tale. 'You *might* have waked
us!' said Dick, crossly.

'We would have if there had been anything much
to see,' said George. 'But there was only just the light from
a lantern, and nothing else except that we thought we
heard the sound of voices.'

When the tide was low enough the children and
Timothy set off over the rocks to the wreck. They clambered up and stood on the slanting, slippery deck. They
looked towards the locker where the little trunk had stood.
The door of the locker was shut this time.

Julian slid down towards it and tried to pull it open.
Someone had stuffed a piece of wood in to keep the locker
from swinging open. Julian pulled it out. Then the door
opened easily.

'Anything else in there?' said George, stepping carefully over the slimy deck to Julian.

'Yes,' said Julian. 'Look! Tins of food! And cups and
plates and things – just as if someone was going to come

and live on the island too! Isn't it funny? The trunk is
still here too, locked as before. And here are some candles
and a little lamp – and a bundle of rags. Whatever *ar*
they here for?'

It really was a puzzle. Julian frowned for a few
minutes, trying to think it out.

'It looks as if someone is going to come and stay on
the island for a bit – probably to wait there and take in
whatever goods are going to be smuggled. Well – we shall
be on the look-out for them, day or night!'

They left the wreck, feeling excited. They had a fine
hiding-place in their cave – no one could possibly find
them there. And, from their hiding-place they could
watch anyone coming to and from the wreck, and, from
the wreck, to the island.

'What about our cove, where we put our boat?'
said George, suddenly. 'They might use that cove, you
know – if they came in a boat. It's rather dangerous to
reach the island from the wreck, if anyone tried to get
to the rocky beach near-by.'

'Well – if anyone came to our cove, they'd see our
boat,' said Dick, in alarm. 'We'd better hide it, hadn't
we?'

'How?' said Anne, thinking that it would be a difficult
thing to hide a boat as big as theirs.

'Don't know,' said Julian. 'We'll go and have a look.'

All four and Timmy went off to the cove into which
they had rowed their boat. The boat was pulled high up
out of reach of the waves. George explored the cove
well, and then had an idea. 'Do you think we could pull
the boat round this big rock? It would just about hide

t, though anyone going round the rock would see it at
nce.'

The others thought it would be worth while trying,
nyway. So, with much panting and puffing, they hauled
he boat round the rock, which almost completely hid
er.

'Good!' said George, going down into the cove to see
f very much of the boat showed. 'A bit of her does show
till. Let's drape it with seaweed!'

So they draped the prow of the boat with all the
eaweed they could find at hand, and after that, unless

anyone went deliberately round the big rock, the boat really was not noticeable at all.

'Good!' said Julian, looking at his watch. 'I say – it's long past tea-time – and, you know, whilst we've been doing all this with the boat, we quite forgot to have some one on the look-out post on the cliff-top. What idiots we are!'

'Well, I don't expect anything has happened since we've been away from the cave,' said Dick, putting a fine big bit of seaweed on the prow of the boat, as a last touch. 'I bet the smugglers will only come at night.'

'I dare say you're right,' said Julian. 'I think we'd better keep a look-out at night, too. The look-out could take rugs up to the cliff-top and curl up there.'

'Timmy could be with whoever is keeping watch,' said Anne, 'Then if the look-out goes to sleep by mistake, Timmy would growl and wake them up if he saw anything.'

'You mean, when *you* go to sleep,' said Dick, grinning. 'Come on – let's get back to the cave and have some tea.'

And then Timothy suddenly began to growl again!

Chapter Fifteen

WHO IS ON THE ISLAND?

'Sh!' said Julian, at once. 'Get down behind this bush, quick, everyone!'

They had left the cove and were walking towards the castle when Timmy growled. Now they all crouched behind a mass of brambles, their hearts beating fast.

'Don't growl, Timmy,' said George, in Timothy's nearest ear. He stopped at once, but he stood stiff and quivering, on the watch.

Julian peeped through the bush, parting the brambles and scratching his hands. He could just see somebody in the courtyard – one person – two persons – maybe three. He strained his eyes to try and see, but even as he looked, they disappeared.

'I believe they've moved those big stones over the entrance to the dungeons, and have gone down there,' he whispered. 'Stay here, and I'll creep out a bit and see. I won't let anyone spot me.'

He came back and nodded. 'Yes – they've gone down the dungeons. Do you think they can be the smugglers? Do you suppose they are storing their smuggled goods down there? It would be a marvellous place, of course.'

'Let's get back to the cave whilst they are underground,' said George. 'I'm so afraid Timmy will give the game away by barking. He's just bursting himself trying not to make some sort of noise.'

'Come on, then!' said Julian. 'Don't go across the
courtyard — make for the shore and we'll scramble round
it till we get to the cave. Then one of us can pop
up through the hole and hide behind that big gorse-bush
there to see who the smugglers are. They must have come
in by boat either from the wreck, or by rowing cleverly
through the rocks off-shore.'

They got to the cave at last and went in. But no sooner
had Julian shinned up the rope, helped by the others, than
Timothy disappeared! He ran out of the cave whilst the
others' backs were turned, and when George turned
round there was no Timmy to be seen!

'Timmy!' she called in a low voice. 'Timmy! Where
are you?'

But no answer came! Timmy had gone off on his own!
If only the smugglers didn't see him! What a bad dog he
was to do that!

But Timmy had smelt something exciting — he had
smelt a smell he knew — a dog-smell — and he meant to
find the owner of it and bite off his ears and tail!
'Gr-r-r-r-r!' Timmy was not going to allow dogs on *his*
island!

Julian sat close beside the gorse-bush, watching all
round. There was nothing to be seen on the wreck, and
there was no ship out to sea. Probably the boat that had
brought the strangers to the island was hidden down below among the rocks. Julian looked behind him, towards
the castle — and even as he looked, he saw an astonishing
sight!

A dog was sniffing about the bushes not very far away
— and creeping up behind him, all his hackles up, was

Timothy! Timothy was stalking the dog as if he were a cat stalking a rabbit! The other dog suddenly heard him and leapt round, facing Timothy. Timmy flung himself on the dog with a blood-curdling howl, and the dog howled in fright.

Julian watched in horror, not knowing what to do. The two dogs made a fearful noise, especially the other dog whose howls of terror and yelps of rage resounded everywhere.

'This will bring the smugglers up, and they will see Timmy and know there's someone on the island,' thought Julian. 'Oh, blow you, Timmy! – why didn't you stay with George and keep quiet?'

From the walls of the ruined castle came three figures, running pell-mell to see what was happening to their dog – and Julian stared at them in the very greatest amazement – for the three people were no other than Mr. Stick, Mrs. Stick and Edgar!

'Golly!' said Julian, crawling round the bush to get to the hole quickly. 'They've come after us! They've guessed we've gone here and they've come to look for us, the beasts, to make us go back! Well, they won't find us! But oh, what a pity Timmy's given the show away!'

There came a shrill whistle from down below him. It was George, who, hearing the row from the dogs, was feeling worried, and had sent out her piercing whistle for Timmy. It was a whistle the dog always obeyed, and he let go his hold of the dog and shot off to the cliff-top at once, just as the three Sticks arrived on the scene, and picked up their bleeding, whining mongrel.

Edgar tore after Timmy, up to the cliff-top. Julian

dropped down to the cave when he spotted Edgar appear
ing. Timmy ran to the hole and dropped bodily down
landing almost on top of Julian. He flung himself o
George.

'Shut up, shut up!' said George, in an urgent whispe
to the excited dog. 'Do you want to give our hiding-plac
away, you idiot?'

Edgar, panting and puffing, arrived on the cliff-top
and was completely amazed to see Timothy apparently
disappear into the solid earth. He hunted about for a
bit, but it was clear that the dog was no longer on the
cliff.

Mr. and Mrs. Stick came up too. 'Where did that dog
go?' shouted Mrs. Stick. 'What was he like?'

'He looked awfully like that horrible dog of the chil
dren's,' said Edgar. His voice could clearly be heard by
everyone down in the cave. The children kept as quiet a
mice.

'But it *couldn't* be!' came Mrs. Stick's voice. 'The
children have gone home – we saw them, *and* the dog too
making off towards the railway. It must be some sort o
stray dog left here by a tripper.'

'Well, where is he, then?' said Mr. Stick's hoarse voice
'Can't see no dog anywheres about now.'

'He disappeared into the earth,' said Edgar, in a surprised voice.

Mr. Stick made a rude and scornful noise. 'You tel
lovely tales, you do,' he said. 'Disappeared into the earth
What next? Fell over the cliff, I should think. Well, he go
his teeth into poor Tinker good and proper. My word
if I see that dog, I'll shoot him!'

'He might have some hiding-place about this cliff,' said Mrs. Stick. 'Let's have a look!'

The children sat as quiet as mice. George with a warning hand on Timmy's collar. They could hear that the Sticks were really very near. Julian expected one of them to fall down the hole at any moment!

But mercifully they didn't happen on the hole that led down to the cave. They stood quite near to it, though, whilst they were discussing the problem.

'If it's the children's dog, then those tiresome kids must have come to this island, instead of going home,' said Mrs. Stick. 'That would upset our plan all right! We shall have to find out. I'll have no peace till I know.'

'We can soon find out,' said Mr. Stick. 'No need to worry about that. Their boat will be here somewhere – and they'll all be about, too! It's impossible for four children, a dog and a boat to be hidden on this small island once anyone starts hunting for them! Edgar, you go round that way. Clara, you get along round about the castle. They may be hiding somewhere in the ruins. I'll have a look about here.'

The children crouched together in the cave. How they hoped that their boat would not be found! How they hoped that no one would find any traces of them at all! Timmy growled softly, wishing that he could go and find that Stinker-dog again! It had been lovely to bite his ears hard.

Edgar was half-scared of finding the children, and a good deal more scared of coming up against Timmy somewhere. So he did not make much of a search for either the children or the boat. He went into the cove

where the boat had been pulled up, and although he saw
traces where the vessel had been hauled up, barely
smoothed out by the sea-water at high-tide, he did no
notice the seaweedy prow of the boat sticking out round
the rock behind which it was hidden.

'Nothing here!' he called to his mother, who was
going round and about the ruins, looking into every likely
nook. But she found nothing either, and neither did
Mr. Stick.

'Couldn't have been the children's dog,' said Mr. Stick
at last. 'They'd be here if he was, and so would their boat
—but there's no sign of them at all. That dog must have
been some wild stray. Have to look out for him, no doubt
about it. Gone wild, I should think.'

The children relaxed after about an hour, thinking
that the Sticks must have given up looking for them.
They boiled the kettle to make some tea, and Anne began
to cut some sandwiches. Timmy was tied up in case he
wandered out again to look for Stinker.

They ate their tea quietly, not speaking above a
whisper. 'The Sticks haven't come here to look for us
after all,' said Julian. 'It's quite plain from what they say
that they thought we had gone to catch the train home,
taking George and Timmy with us.'

'Then what are they here for?' demanded George
fiercely. 'It's *our* island! They've no right here. Let's go
and turn them off! They're scared of Timmy. We'll take
him with us and say we'll set him on to them if they don't
clear out.'

'No, George,' said Julian. 'Do be sensible. We don't
want them rushing off and telling your father we are here

or he may lose his temper and come flying home to order us back. And – there's another thing I've thought of.'

'What?' asked the others, seeing Julian's eyes gleam in the way they did when he had an idea.

'Well,' said Julian, 'don't you think it's possible that the Sticks are something to do with the smugglers? Don't you think they may come here to take off smuggled goods, or to hide them till they can take them off in safety? Mr. Stick is a sailor, isn't he? He would know all about smuggling. I bet he's in the pay of the smugglers all right.'

'I believe you're right!' said George, in excitement. 'Well – we'll wait till the Sticks have gone, and then we'll go down into the dungeons and see if they've hidden anything there! We'll find out their little game and stop it! It will be terribly thrilling, won't it?'

Chapter Sixteen

THE STICKS GET A FRIGHT

B‍ut the Sticks didn't go! The children peeped out of the spy-hole at the top of the cave-roof every now and again, and saw one or other of the Sticks. The evening went on and it began to be dark. Still the Sticks didn't go. Julian ran down to the nearby shore and discovered a small boat there. So the Sticks had managed to find their way round the island, rowed near the wreck, maybe landed on it too, and then come to the shore, cleverly avoiding the rocks they might strike against.

'It looks as if the Sticks have come to stay for the night,' said Julian, gloomily. 'This is going to spoil our stay here, isn't it? We rush away here to escape from the Sticks — and lo and behold! the Sticks are on top of us again. It's too bad.'

'Let's frighten them,' said George, her eyes shining by the light of the one candle in the cave.

'What do you mean?' said Dick, cheering up. He always liked George's ideas, mad as they sometimes were.

'Well, I suppose they must be living down in one of the dungeon rooms, mustn't they?' said George. 'There is no place in the ruins to live in proper shelter, or we'd be there ourselves — and the only other place is down in the dungeons. I wouldn't care to sleep there myself, but I don't suppose the Sticks would mind.'

'Well, what about it?' said Dick. 'What's your idea?'

'Couldn't we creep down, and do a bit of shouting, so that the echoes start up all round?' said George. 'You know how frightening we found the echoes when we first went down into the dungeons. We only had to say one or two words, and the echoes began saying them over and over again shouting them back at us.'

'Oh yes, I remember,' said Anne. 'And wasn't Timmy frightened when he barked! The echoes barked back at him, and he thought there were thousands of dogs hiding down there! He was awfully frightened.'

.'It's a good idea,' said Julian. 'Serve the Sticks right for coming to our island like this! If we can frighten them away, that would be one up to us! Let's do it.'

'What about Timothy?' said Anne. 'Hadn't we better leave him behind?'

'No. He can come and stand at the dungeon entrance to guard it for us,' said George. 'Then if any of the real smugglers happened to come, Timmy could give us warning. I'm not going to leave him behind.'

'Come on, then, let's go now!' said Julian. 'It would be a fine trick to play. It's quite dark, but I've got my torch, and as soon as we are certain that the Sticks are down in the dungeons, we can start to play our joke.'

There was no sign or sound of the Sticks anywhere about. No light of fire or candle was to be seen, no sound of voices to be heard. Either they had gone, or they were below in the dungeons. The stones had been taken from the entrance, so the children felt sure they were down there.

'Now Timmy, you stay quite still and quiet here,'

whispered George to Timmy. 'Bark if anyone comes, but not unless. We're going down into the dungeons.'

'I think perhaps I'll stay up here with Timothy,' said Anne, suddenly. She didn't like the dark look of the dungeon entrance. 'You see, George – Timmy might be frightened or lonely up here by himself.'

The others chuckled. They knew Anne was frightened. Julian squeezed her arm. 'You stay here, then,' he said, kindly. 'You keep old Timmy company.'

Then Julian, George and Dick went down the long flight of steps that led into the deep old dungeons of Kirrin Castle. They had been there the summer before, when they had been seeking for lost treasure; now here they were again!

They crept down the steps and came to the many cellars or dungeons cut out of the rock below the castle. There were scores of those, some big and some small, queer, damp underground rooms in which, maybe, unhappy prisoners had been kept in the olden days.

The children crept down the dark passages. Julian had a piece of white chalk with him, and drew a chalk-line here and there on the rocky walls as he went, so that he might easily find the way back.

Suddenly they heard voices and saw a light. They stopped and whispered softly together in each other's ears.

'They're in that room where we found the treasure last year! That's where they're camping out! What noises shall we make?'

'I'll be a cow,' said Dick. 'I can moo awfully like a cow. I'll be a cow.'

'I'll be a sheep,' said Julian. 'George, you be a horse
You can whinny and hrrrumph just like a horse. Dick
you begin!'

So Dick began. Hidden behind a rocky pillar, he
opened his mouth and mooed dolefully, like a cow in
pain. At once the echoes took up the mooing, magnified it
sent it along all the underground passages, till it seemed
as if a thousand cows had wandered there and were moo
ing together.

'Moo – oo – oo – OOOOOOOO, ooo – oo –
MOOOOOOO!'

The Sticks listened in amazement and fright at the
sudden awful noise.

'What is it, Ma?' said Edgar, almost in tears. Stinker
crouched at the back of the cave, terrified.

'It's cows,' said Mr. Stick, amazed. 'Them there's cows
Can't you hear the moos? But how did cows get to be
here?'

'Nonsense!' said Mrs. Stick, recovering herself a little
'Cows down these caves! You're mad! You'll be telling
me there's sheep next!'

It was funny that she should have said that, for Julian
chose that moment to begin baa-ing like a flock of sheep
His one long, bleating 'baa-baa-aa-aa' was taken up by
the echoes at once, and it seemed suddenly as if hundred
of poor lost sheep were baa-ing their way down the dun
geons!

Mr. Stick jumped to his feet, as white as a sheet.

'Well, if it isn't sheep now!' he said. 'What's up?
What's in these 'ere dungeons? I never did like them.'

'Baa-aa-AAAAAAAAAA!' went the mournful bleat

all round and about. And then George started her whinnying and neighing, just like an impatient horse. The little girl tossed her head in the darkness and arrrumphed exactly like a horse and then she stamped with her foot, and at once the echoes stamped too, sending the whinnying and neighing and stamping into Sticks' cave twenty times louder than George had made them.

Poor Stinker began to whine pitifully. He was frightened almost out of his life. He pressed himself against the door as if he would like to disappear into it. Edgar clutched his mother's arm. 'Let's go up,' he said. 'I can't stay here. There's hundreds of sheep and horses and cows roaming these dungeons, you can hear them. They're not real, but they've got voices and hoofs, and I'm scared of them.'

Mr. Stick went to the door of the room they were in, and shouted loudly.

'Get out, you! Clear out! Whoever you are!'

George giggled. Then she shouted out in a very deep, hoarse voice.

'BE-WARE!' And the echoes thundered out all round. ' 'WARE! 'WARE! 'WARE-ARE-ARE!'

Mr. Stick went back quickly into the cave-room, and lighted another candle. He shut the big wooden door that led into the room. His hands were shaking.

'Queer goings-on,' he said. 'Shan't stay here much longer if we get this kind of thing happening every night.'

Julian, Dick and George were now in such a state of giggle that they could not imitate any more cows, horses

or sheep. George did begin to be a pig, and gave such
realistic snort and grunt that Dick nearly died of laugh
ing. The snorts and grunts were echoed everywhere.

'Come out' gasped Julian, at last. 'I shall burst wit
trying not to laugh. Come out!'

'Come out!' whispered the echoes. 'Come out, ou
out!'

They stumbled out, stuffing hankies into their mouth
as they went, following Julian's chalk-marks easily by th
light of his torch. It was impossible to take the wrong pas
sage if they followed his guiding-lines.

They sat on the dungeon steps with Anne and Timmy
and choked with laughter as they related all they ha
done. 'We heard old Stick yelling to us to clear out,' sai
George, 'and he sounded scared stiff. As for Stinker, w
never heard even the smallest growl from him. I bet th
Sticks will clear off tomorrow after this! It must hav
given them a most terrible fright.'

'Oh, that was grand!' said Julian. 'It was a pity I bega
to laugh. I was just feeling I might trumpet like an ele
phant next. The echoes would like that!'

'Funny the Sticks all staying on the island like this
said Dick, thoughtfully. 'They've left Kirrin Cottage
but they're not looking for us. They must be in leagu
with the smugglers all right. Perhaps that's why Mrs
Stick took the job with your mother, George – to be nea
the island when the time came – when the smuggler
wanted their help.'

'We could really go back to Kirrin Cottage, couldn'
we?' said Anne, who, much as she loved the island, wa
not nearly so keen on it now that the Sticks were there.

'Go back! Leave an adventure just when it's beginning!' said George, scornfully. 'How silly you are, Anne. Go back if you want to – but I'm sure nobody will go with you.'

'Oh, Anne will stay with us all right,' said Julian, knowing that Anne would feel hurt at the suggestion she should leave them. 'It will be the Sticks who have to go, don't worry!'

'Let's go back to the cave,' said Anne, thinking longingly of its safety and bright little candle. They got up and made their way across the courtyard to the little wall that ran round the castle. They climbed over it and turned their steps to the cliff. Julian switched on his torch when he thought it was safe, for it was impossible to see clearly in the dark, and he did not want any of them to fall down the hole, instead of climbing down properly by the rope.

Julian stood by the hole at last, shining his torch so that the others might climb down the rope in safety, one by one. He glanced up, looking over the dark sea, as he stood there, and then stared intently.

There was a light out to sea, and it was signalling. It must have seen his torchlight! Julian watched, wondering if it was a ship that was signalling, and how far out it was, and why it was signalling.

'Perhaps they're going to put more stuff into the old wreck for the Sticks to find,' he thought. 'I wonder if they are. How I'd like to find out – but it would be dangerous to go there in daylight in case the Sticks see us.'

The signalling went on for a long time, as if a message was being flashed. Julian could not for the life of him make out what it was. It simply looked like the flash-flash-

flash of a lantern to him. But it must mean a signal o
message of some sort to the Sticks.

'Well, they won't get it tonight!' thought Julian, with
a chuckle, when at last the signalling stopped. 'I rathe
think the Stick family will stay where they are tonight
too scared of sheep and cows and horses rushing abou
those dungeons!'

Julian was quite right – the Sticks did stay where they
were! Nothing would get them out of their underground
room till morning.

Chapter Seventeen

A SHOCK FOR EDGAR

THE children slept well that night, and as Timothy did
not growl at all, they were sure that nothing important
could have happened. They had a fine breakfast of
tongue, tinned peaches, bread and butter, golden syrup
and ginger-beer.

'That's the end of the ginger-beer, I'm afraid,' said
Julian, regretfully. 'I must say ginger-beer is a gorgeous
drink – seems to go with simply everything.'

'That was the nicest meal I've ever had,' said Anne. 'It
really was. We do have lovely meals on Kirrin Island. I
wonder if the Sticks are having nice meals too.'

'You bet they are!' said Dick. 'I expect they have ran-
sacked Aunt Fanny's cupboards and taken the best they
can find.'

'Oh, the beasts!' said George, her eyes flashing. 'I
never thought of that – they may have robbed the house
and taken all kinds of things.'

'They probably have,' said Julian, and he frowned.
'I say, I never thought of that, somehow. How awful,
George, if your mother came back, feeling ill and weak,
and found half her belongings gone!'

'Oh dear!' said Anne, dismayed. 'George, wouldn't
that be dreadful?'

'Yes,' said George, looking very angry. 'I would believe
anything of those Sticks! If they have the cheek to come

to our island and live here, they've the cheek to steal from my mother's house. I wish we could find out.'

'They could have brought quite a lot of things away in their boat,' said Julian. 'They must have come here by boat. If they did bring stolen goods, they must have put them somewhere – down in the dungeons, I suppose.'

'We might have a look round and see if we can spy anything, without the Sticks seeing us,' suggested Dick.

'Let's have a look round now,' said George, who always liked doing things at once. 'Anne, you do the washing up and tidy our cave-house for us, will you?'

Anne was torn between wanting to go with the others and longing to play 'house' again. She did so love arranging everything and making the beds and tidying up the cave. In the end she said she would stay and the others could go.

So up the rope they went. Timothy stayed with Anne because they were afraid he might bark. Anne tied him up, and he whined a little, but did not make a terrible noise.

The other three lay flat on the cliff-top, looking down on the ruined castle. There seemed to be no one about, but, even as they watched, the three Sticks appeared, apparently coming up from the dungeons. They seemed glad to be in the sunshine, and the children were not surprised, for the dungeons were so cold and dark.

The Sticks looked all round. Stinker kept close to Mr Stick, his tail well down.

'They're looking for the cows and sheep and horse they heard down in the dungeons last night!' whispered Dick to Julian.

The Sticks spoke together for a minute or two, and
then went off in the direction of the shore that faced the
wreck. Edgar went to the room in which the children
had first planned to sleep – the one whose roof had fallen
in.

'I'm going to stalk the two Sticks,' whispered Julian to
the others. 'You two see what Edgar is up to.'

Julian disappeared, keeping behind bushes as he
watched where the Sticks went, and followed them.
George and Dick went cautiously and quietly over the
cliff to the castle in the middle of the little island. They
could hear Edgar whistling. Stinker was running about
the courtyard of the castle.

Edgar appeared out of the ruined room, carrying a
pile of cushions, which had evidently been stored there.
George went red with rage and clutched Dick's arm
fiercely.

'Mother's best cushions!' she whispered. 'Oh, the
beasts!'

Dick felt angry too. It was quite plain that the Sticks
had helped themselves to anything handy when they had
left Kirrin Cottage. He picked up a clod of earth, took
careful aim, and flung it into the air. It fell between
Edgar and Stinker, breaking into a shower of earth.

Edgar dropped the cushions, and looked up into the
air in fright. It was plain that he thought something had
fallen from the sky. George picked up another clod, took
aim, and flung it high into the air. It fell all over Stinker,
and the dog gave a yelp, and scuttled down the hole that
led into the dungeons.

Edgar looked up into the sky and then all round and

about him, his mouth wide open. What could be hap
pening? Dick waited until he was looking in the opposi
direction, and then once more sent a big clod into th
air. It fell into bits and scattered itself all over the startle
Edgar.

Then Dick gave one of his realistic moos, exactly like
cow in pain, and Edgar stood rooted to the spot, almo
frightened out of his skin. Those cows again! Whe
were they?

Dick mooed again, and Edgar gave a yell, found h
feet, and almost fell down the dungeon steps. He di
appeared with a dismal howl, leaving behind all th
cushions on the ground.

'Quick!' said Dick, jumping to his feet. 'He won't b
back for a few minutes, anyhow. He'll be too scared. Let
grab the cushions and bring them here. I don't see wh
the Sticks should use them down in those awful old du
geons.'

The two children raced to the courtyard, picked u
the cushions and raced back to their hiding-place. Di
looked across to the room where Edgar had brought the
from.

'What about slipping across there and seeing what el
they've stored away?' he said. 'I don't see why they shou
be allowed to have anything that isn't theirs.'

'I'll go across, and you keep watch by the dunge
entrance,' said George. 'You've only got to moo again
you see Edgar, and he'll run for miles.'

'Right,' said Dick, with a grin, and went swiftly to th
flight of steps that led underground to the dungeor
There was no sign of Edgar at all, nor of Stinker.

George went to the ruined room and gazed round in nger. Yes, the Sticks certainly *had* helped themselves to er mother's things, no doubt about that! There were lankets and silver and all kinds of food. Mrs. Stick ust have gone into the big cupboard under the stairs nd taken out various things stored there for weekly use.

George ran to Dick. 'There are heaps of our things!' e said, in a fierce whisper. 'Come and help me to get em. We'll see if we can take them all before Edgar ppears, or the Sticks come back.'

Just as they were whispering together, they heard a w whistle. They looked round, and saw Julian coming ong. He joined them.

'The Sticks have rowed off to the wreck,' he said. hey've got an old boat somewhere down among those cks. Old Pa Stick must be a good sailor to be able to ke the boat in and out of those awful hidden rocks.'

'Oh, then we've got time to do what we want to do,' id Dick, pleased. He hurriedly told Julian of the things eorge had seen in the ruined room.

'Awful thieves!' said Julian, indignantly. 'They don't ean to go back to Kirrin Cottage, that's plain. They've t some business on with the smugglers here – and when at is done they'll go off with all their stolen goods, join ship somewhere, and get off scot-free.'

'No, they won't,' said George at once. 'We are going get everything and take it to the cave! Dick's going to ep watch for Edgar at the cave entrance, and you and Julian, can quickly carry the things away. We can op them down the hole into the cave.'

'Hurry then!' said Julian. 'We must do it before the

Sticks return, and I don't expect they'll be long. They've probably gone to fetch the trunk and anything else in the wreck. You know I saw a light out to sea last night – maybe that's a signal that the smugglers were leaving something in the wreck for the Sticks to fetch.'

George and Julian ran to the ruined room, piled their arms with the goods there, and then ran to hide them on the cliff, ready to take them to the hole when they had time. It looked as if the Sticks had just taken whatever was easiest to lay their hands on. They had even got the kitchen clock!

Edgar did not appear at all, so Dick had nothing to do but sit by the steps of the dungeon and watch the others. After some time Julian and George gave a sigh of relief and beckoned to Dick. He left his place and went to join them.

'We've got everything now,' said Julian. 'I'm just going to the cliff-edge to see if the Sticks are returning yet. If they're not we'll all carry the things to the hole in the roof of the cave.'

He soon returned. 'I can see their boat tied to the wreck,' he said. 'We're safe for some while yet. Come on, let's get the things to safety! This really is a bit of luck!'

They carried the things to the hole and called down to Anne. 'Anne! We've got tons of things to put down the hole. Stand by to catch!'

Soon all kinds of things came down the hole into the cave! Anne was most astonished. The silver and any thing that might be hurt by a fall was first wrapped up in the blankets, and then let down by a rope.

'My goodness!' said Anne. 'This cave will *really* look

like a house soon, when I have arranged all these things
too!'

Just as they were finishing their job the children heard
voices in the distance.

'The Sticks are back!' said Julian, and looked cautiously over the cliff-top. He was right. They had returned
to their boat, and were even now on their way back to the
castle, carrying the trunk from the wreck.

'Let's follow them, and see what happens when they
find everything gone,' grinned Julian. 'Come on, everyone!'

They wriggled over the cliff on their tummies, and
came to a clump of bushes behind which they could hide

and watch. The Sticks put the trunk down, and looked round for Edgar. But Edgar was nowhere to be seen.

'Where's that boy?' said Mrs. Stick, impatiently. 'He's had plenty of time to do everything. Edgar! Edgar. Edgar!'

Mr. Stick went to the ruined room and peeped inside. He came back to Mrs. Stick.

'He's taken everything down,' he said. 'He must be down in the dungeon. That room's quite empty.'

'I told him to come up and sit in the sun when he'd finished,' said Mrs. Stick. ' 'Tisn't healthy down in them dungeons. EDGAR!'

This time Edgar heard, and his head appeared, looking out of the entrance to the dungeon. He looked extremely scared.

'Come on up!' said Mrs. Stick. 'You've got all the things down, and you'd better stay up here in the sunshine now.'

'I'm scared,' said Edgar. 'I'm not staying up here alone.'

'Why not?' said Mr. Stick, astonished.

'It's them cows again!' said poor Edgar. 'Hundreds of them, Pa, all a-mooing round me, and throwing things at me. They're dangerous animals, they are, and I'm not coming up here alone!'

Chapter Eighteen

AN UNEXPECTED PRISONER

THE Sticks stared at Edgar as if he was mad.

'Cows throwing things?' said Mrs. Stick at last. 'What do you mean by that? Cows don't throw anything.'

'These ones did,' said Edgar, and then began to exaggerate in order to make his parents sympathize with him. They were dreadful cows, they were – hundreds of them – with horns as long as reindeer, and awful mooing voices. And they threw things at me and Tinker. Proper scared he was, and so was I. I dropped the cushions I was taking down, and rushed away to hide.'

'Where are the cushions?' said Mr. Stick, looking round. 'I can't see no cushions. I suppose you'll tell us he cows ate them.'

'Didn't you take everything down into the dungeons?' demanded Mrs. Stick. 'Because that room's empty now. There's not a thing in it.'

'I didn't take nothing down at all,' said Edgar, coming cautiously out of the dungeon entrance. 'I dropped the cushions just about where you're standing. What's happened to them?'

'Look 'ere!' said Mr. Stick, in amazement. ' 'Oo's been ere since we've been gone? Someone's taken them ushions and everything else too. Where have they put hem?'

'Pa, it was them cows,' said Edgar, looking all round a if he expected to see cows walking off with cushion and silver and blankets.

'Shut up about them cows,' said Mrs. Stick, suddenl losing her temper. 'For one thing there aren't any cow on this island, and that we do know, for we looked all ove it this morning. What we heard last night must hav been queer sort of echoes rumbling round. No, my boy there's something funny about all this. Looks as if ther *is* somebody on the island!'

A dismal howl came echoing up from below the ground It was Stinker, terrified at being alone below, and no daring to come up.

'Poor lamb!' said Mrs. Stick, who seemed much fonde of Stinker than of anyone else.

'What's up with him?'

Stinker let out an even more doleful howl, and Mrs Stick hurried down the steps to go to him. Mr. Stick followed her, and Edgar lost no time in going after them

'Quick!' said Julian, standing up. 'Come with me Dick. We may just have time to get that trunk! Run!'

The two boys ran quickly down to the courtyard of th ruined castle. Each took a handle of the small trunk, an lifted it between them. They staggered back to Georg with it.

'We'll take it to the cave,' whispered Julian. 'You sta here a few minutes and see what happens.'

The boys went over the cliff with the trunk. Georg flattened herself behind her bush and watched. M Stick appeared again in a few minutes, and looked roun for the trunk. His mouth fell open in astonishment whe

he saw that it was gone. He yelled down the entrance to
the dungeon.

'Clara! The trunk's gone!'

Mrs. Stick was already on her way up, with Stinker
close beside her and Edgar just behind. She climbed out
and stared round.

'Gone?' she said, in enormous surprise. 'Gone? Where's
it gone?'

'That's what *I'd* like to know!' said Mr. Stick. 'We
leave it here a few minutes – and then it goes. Walks off
by itself – just like all the other things!'

'Look here! There's someone on this island,' said Mrs.
Stick. 'And I'm going to find out who it is. Got your gun,
Pa?'

'I have,' said Mr. Stick, slapping his belt. 'You get a
good stout stick too, and we'll take Tinker. If we don't
ferret out whoever's trying to spoil our plans, my name's
not Stick!'

George slipped away quietly to warn the others. Before she slid down the rope into the cave, she pulled several
bramble sprays across the hole. She dropped down to the
floor of the cave, and told the others what had happened.

Julian had been trying to open the trunk, but it was
still locked. He looked up as George panted out her tale.

'We'll be all right here so long as no one falls down that
hole in the roof!' he said. 'Now keep quiet everyone, and
don't you dare to growl, Timmy!'

Nothing was heard for some time, and then Stinker's
bark came in the distance. 'Quiet now,' said Julian. 'They
are near here.'

The Sticks were up on the cliff once more, searching carefully behind every bush. They came to the great bush behind which the children often hid, and saw the flattened grass there.

'Someone's been here,' said Mr. Stick. 'I wonder if they're in the middle of this bush – it's thick enough to hide half an army! I'll try and force my way in, Clara, while you stand by with my gun.'

Edgar wandered off by himself whilst this was happening, feeling certain that nobody would be foolish enough to live in the middle of such a prickly bush. He walked across the cliff – and then, to his awful horror, he found himself falling! His legs disappeared into a hole, he clutched at some thorny sprays but could not save himself. Down he went, and down and down – and down – crash!

Edgar had fallen down the hole in the roof of the cave. He suddenly appeared before the children's startled eyes, and landed in a heap on the soft sand. Timmy at once pounced on him with a fearsome growl, but George pulled him off just in time.

Edgar was half-stunned with fright and his fall. He lay on the floor of the cave, groaning, his eyes shut. The children stared at him and then at one another. For a few moments they were completely taken aback and didn't know what to do or say. Timmy growled ferociously – so ferociously that Edgar opened his eyes in fright. He stared round at the four children and their dog in the utmost surprise and horror.

He opened his mouth to yell for help, but at once found Julian's large hand over it. 'Yell just once and

Timmy shall have a bite out of any part of you he likes!' said Julian, in a voice as ferocious as Timothy's growl. 'See? Like to try it? Timmy's waiting to bite.'

'I shan't yell,' said Edgar, speaking in such a low whisper that the others could hardly hear him. 'Keep that dog off. I shan't yell.'

George spoke to Timothy. 'Now you listen, Timothy – if this boy shouts, you just go for him! Lie here by him and show him your big teeth. Bite him wherever you like if he yells.'

'Woof!' said Timmy, looking really pleased. He lay down by Edgar, and the boy tried to move away. But Timmy came nearer every time he moved.

Edgar looked round at the children. 'What you doing on this island?' he said. 'We thought you'd gone home.'

'It's *our* island!' said George, in a very fierce voice. 'We've every right to be on it if we want to – but you have no right at all. None! What are you and your father and mother here for?'

'Don't know,' said Edgar, looking sulky.

'You'd better tell us,' said Julian. 'We know you're in league with smugglers.'

Edgar looked startled. 'Smugglers?' he said. 'I didn't know that. Pa and Ma don't tell me nothing. I don't want nothing to do with smugglers.'

'Don't you know *any*-thing?' said Dick. 'Don't you know why you've come to Kirrin Island?'

'I don't know nothing,' said Edgar, in an injured tone. 'Pa and Ma are mean to me. They never tell me nothing. I do as I'm told, that's all. I don't know nothing about smugglers, I tell you that.'

It was quite plain to the children that Edgar really did not know anything of the reasons for his parents coming to the island. 'Well, I'm not surprised they don't let Spotty-Face into their secrets,' said Julian. 'He'd blab them if he could, I bet. Anyway, we know it's smuggling they're mixed up in.'

'You let me go,' said Edgar, sullenly. 'You got no right to keep me here.'

'We're not going to let you go,' said George at once. 'You're our prisoner now. If we let you go back to your parents, you'd tell them all about us, and we don't want them to know we're here. We're going to spoil their pretty plans, you see.'

Edgar saw. He saw quite a lot of things. He felt rather sick. 'Was it you that took the cushions and things?' he said.

'Oh no, dear Edgar,' said Dick. 'It was the cows, wasn't it? Don't you remember how you told your mother about the hundreds of cows that mooed at you and threw things and stole the cushions you dropped? Surely you haven't forgotten your cows already?'

'Funny, aren't you?' said Edgar, sulkily. 'What you going to do with me? I won't stay here, that's flat.'

'But you will, Spotty-Face,' said Julian. 'You will stay here till we let you go – and that won't be till we've cleared up this little smuggling mystery. And let me warn you that any nonsense on your part will be punished by Timmy.'

'Lot of beasts you are,' said Edgar, seeing that he could do nothing but obey the four children. 'My Pa and Ma won't half be furious with you.'

His Ma and Pa were feeling extremely astonished. There had, of course, been nobody hiding in the big thick bush, and when Mr. Stick had wriggled out, scratched and bleeding, he had looked round for Edgar. And Edgar was not to be seen.

'Where's that dratted boy?' he said, and shouted for him. 'Edgar! ED-GAR!'

But Edgar did not answer. The Sticks spent a very long time looking for Edgar, both above ground and underground. Mrs. Stick was convinced that poor Edgar was lost in the dungeons, and she tried to send Stinker to find him. But Stinker only went as far as the first cave. He remembered the peculiar noises of the night before and was not at all keen on exploring the dungeons.

Julian turned his attention to the little trunk, once Edgar had been dealt with. 'I'm going to open this somehow,' he said. 'I'm sure it's got smuggled goods in, though goodness knows what.'

'You'll have to smash the locks then,' said Dick. Julian got a small rock and tried to smash the two locks. He managed to wrench one open after a while, and then the other gave way too. The children threw back the lid.

On the top was a child's blanket, embroidered with white rabbits. Julian pulled it off, expecting to see the smuggled goods below. But to his astonishment there were a child's clothes!

He pulled them out. There were two blue jerseys, a blue skirt, some vests and knickers and a warm coat. At the bottom of the trunk were some dolls and a teddy bear!

'Golly!' said Julian, in amazement. 'What are all these

for? Why did the Sticks bring these to the island – and why did the smugglers hide them in the wreck? It's a puzzler!'

Edgar appeared to be as astonished as the rest. He too had expected valuable goods of some kind. George and Anne pulled out the dolls. They were lovely ones. Anne cuddled them up to her. She loved dolls, though George scorned them.

'Who do they belong to?' she said. 'Oh won't she be sad not to have them? Julian, isn't it funny? *Why* should anyone bring a trunk full of clothes and dolls to Kirrin Island?'

Chapter Nineteen

A SCREAM IN THE NIGHT

NOBODY could even guess the answers to Anne's surprised questions. The children stared into the trunk and puzzled over it. It seemed such a funny thing to smuggle. They remembered the other things in the wreck too – the tins of food. They were queer things to smuggle into the island. There didn't seem any point in it.

'Funny,' said Dick, at last. 'It beats me. There's no doubt that queer things are afoot here, or the Sticks wouldn't be hanging around our island. And we've seen signals from a ship out to sea. Something's going on. We thought if we opened this trunk it might help us – but it's only made the mystery deeper.'

Just then the voices of the two parent Sticks could be heard shouting for Edgar. But Edgar did not dare to shout back. Timmy's nose was poked against his leg. He might be nipped at any time. Timmy growled every now and again to remind Edgar that he was still there.

'Do you know anything about the ship that signals to this island at night?' asked Julian, turning to Edgar.

The boy shook his head. 'Never heard of no signals,' he said. 'I just heard my mother saying that she expected the *Roamer* tonight, but I don't know what she meant.'

'The *Roamer*?' said George, at once. 'What's that – a man – or a boat – or what?'

'I don't know,' said Edgar. 'I'd only have got a clip on he ear if I'd asked. Find out yourself.'

'We will,' said Julian, grimly. 'We'll watch out for the *Roamer* tonight! Thanks for the information.'

The children spent a quiet and rather boring day in the cave – all but Anne, who had plenty of things to arrange gain. Really, the cave looked most home-like when she had finished! She put the blankets on the bed, and used he rugs as carpets. So the cave really looked most imposing!

Edgar was not allowed to go out of the cave, and Timothy didn't leave him for a moment. He slept most of the time, complaining that 'them cows and things' had frightened him so much the night before that he'd not been able to sleep a wink.

The others discussed their plans in low voices. They decided to keep watch on the cliff-top, two and two together, that night. They would wait and see what happened. If the *Roamer* came, they would hurriedly make fresh plans then.

The sun sank. The night came up dark over the sea. Edgar snored softly, after a very good supper of sardines, pressed beef sandwiches, tinned apricots and tinned milk. Anne and Dick went up to keep the first watch. It was about half-past ten.

At half-past twelve Julian and George climbed up the knotted rope and joined the other two. They had nothing to report. They went down into the cave, got into their comfortable beds and went to sleep. Edgar was snoring away in his corner, Timmy still on guard.

Julian and George looked out to sea, watching for any

sign of a ship. The moon was up that night, and thing
were not quite so dark. Suddenly they heard low voices
and saw shadowy figures down by the rocks below.

'The two Sticks,' whispered Julian. 'Going to row ou
to the wreck again, I suppose.'

There was the splash of oars, and the children saw
boat move out over the water. At the same time George
nudged Julian violently and pointed out to sea. A ligh
was being shown a good way out, from a ship that th
children could barely see. Then the moon went behin
a cloud, and they could see nothing for some time.

They watched breathlessly. Was that shadowy shi
a good way out the *Roamer*? Or was the owner of it th
'Roamer'? Were the smugglers at work tonight?

'There's another boat coming – look!' said George. 'I
must be coming from that ship out to sea. Now the moo
has come out again, you can just see it. It is going to th
old wreck. It must be a meeting-place, I should think.

Then, most irritatingly, the moon went behind a clou
again, and remained there so long that the children grev
impatient. At last it sailed out again and lighted up th
water.

'Both boats are leaving the wreck now,' said Julian ex
citedly. 'They've had their meeting – and passed over th
smuggled goods, I suppose – and now one boat is return
ing to the ship, and the other, the Sticks' boat, is coming
back here with the goods. We'll follow the Sticks when
they get back and see where they put the goods.'

After a long time the Sticks' boat came to shore again
The children could not see anything then, but presently
they saw the Sticks going back towards the castle. Mr

Stick carried what looked like a large bundle, flung over his shoulder. They could not see if Mrs. Stick carried anything.

The Sticks went into the courtyard of the castle, and came to the dungeon entrance. 'They're taking the smuggled goods down there,' whispered Julian to George. The children were now watching from behind a nearby wall. 'We'll go back and tell the others, and make some more plans. We must somehow or other get those goods ourselves, and take them back to the mainland and get in touch with the police!'

Just then a scream rang out in the night. It was a high-pitched, terrified scream, and frightened the watching children very much. They had no idea where it came from.

'Quick! It must be Anne!' said Julian, and the two ran as fast as they could to the hole that led down to the cave. They dropped down the rope and Julian looked round the quiet cave anxiously. What had happened to Anne to make her scream like that?

But Anne was peacefully asleep on her bed, and so was Dick. Edgar still snored and Timmy watched, his eyes gleaming green.

'Funny,' said Julian, still startled. 'Awfully queer. Who screamed like that? It couldn't possibly have been Anne – because if she had screamed in her sleep like that, she would have wakened the others.'

'Well, who screamed, then?' said George, feeling rather scared. 'Wasn't it weird, Julian? I didn't like it. It was somebody who was awfully frightened. But who could it be?'

They woke Dick and Anne and told them about the strange scream. Anne was very startled. Dick was interested to hear that two boats had met at the wreck and that the Sticks had brought back smuggled goods of some sort, and taken them down into the dungeons.

'We'll get those tomorrow, somehow!' he said, cheerfully. 'We'll have good fun.'

'Why did you think it was me screaming?' asked Anne. 'Did you think it was a girl's scream?'

'Yes. It sounded like the scream you give when one of us jumps out at you suddenly,' said Julian. 'A proper little girl's scream – not a yell, like a boy gives.'

'It's funny,' said Anne. She cuddled down into her bed again, and George got in beside her.

'Oh Anne!' said George, in disgust, 'you've got our bed simply *full* of those dolls – and that teddy bear is here too! You really are a baby!'

'No, I'm not,' said Anne. 'The dolls and the bear are babies – they are frightened and lonely because they're not with the little girl they belong to. So I had them in bed with me instead! I'm sure the little girl would be glad.'

'The little girl!' said Julian, slowly. 'We thought we heard a little girl scream tonight – we found a small trunk full of a little girl's clothes, and a little girl's dolls. What does it all mean?'

There was a silence – and then Anne spoke excitedly. 'I know! The smuggled goods are a little girl! They've stolen a little girl away – and these are her dolls, and those over there are her clothes that were stolen at the same time, for her to dress in and play with. The little girl's here, on this island now – you heard her scream tonight.

when those horrid Sticks carried her down into the dungeons!'

'Well – I do believe Anne has hit on the right idea,' said Julian. 'Clever little girl, Anne! I think you're right. It isn't smugglers who are using this island – it's kidnappers!'

'What are kidnappers?' said Anne.

'People who steal away children or grown-ups and hide them somewhere till a large sum of money is paid out for them,' explained Julian. 'It's called a ransom. Till the ransom is paid, the prisoner is held by the captors.'

'Well, that's what's happened here then!' said George. 'I bet it has! Some poor little rich girl has been stolen away – and brought to the wreck by boat from some ship – and taken over by those horrible Sticks. Wicked creatures!'

'And we heard the poor little thing scream just as she was taken down underground,' said George. 'Julian, we've got to rescue her.'

'Yes, of course,' said Julian. 'We will, never fear! We'll rescue her tomorrow.'

Edgar woke up and joined in the conversation suddenly. 'What you talking about?' he said. 'Rescue who?'

'Never you mind,' said Julian.

George nudged him and whispered.

'All I hope is that Mrs. Stick is feeling as upset about losing her dear Edgar as the mother of the little girl,' she said.

'Tomorrow we find the little girl somehow, and take her away,' said Julian. 'I expect the Sticks will be on guard, but we'll find a way.'

'I'm tired now,' said George, lying down. 'Let's go to
sleep. We'll wake up nice and fresh. Oh Anne, do put
these dolls your side. I'm lying on at least three.'

Anne took the dolls and the bear and arranged them
on her side of the bed. 'Don't feel lonely,' George heard
her say. 'I'll look after you all right till you go back to
your own mistress. Sleep tight!'

Soon they all slept – all but Timothy, who lay with
one eye open all night long. There was no need to put
anyone on guard whilst Timmy was there. He was the
best guardian they could have.

Chapter Twenty

A RESCUE – AND A NEW PRISONER!

THE next day Julian was awake early and went up the
rope to the cliff-top to see if the Sticks were about. He saw
them coming up the steps that led from the dungeons.
Mrs. Stick looked pale and worried.

'We've got to find our Edgar,' she kept saying to Mr.
Stick. 'I tell you we've got to find our Edgar. He's not
down in the dungeons. That I do know. We've yelled ourselves hoarse down there.'

'And he's not on the island,' said Mr. Stick. 'We hunted
all over it yesterday. I think whoever was here then, took
our goods, caught Edgar, and made off with him and
everything else in their boat. That's what I think.'

'Well, they've taken him to the mainland then,' said
Mrs. Stick. 'We'd better take our boat and go back there
and ask a few questions. What I'd like to know is – who
is it messing about here and interfering with our plans?
It makes me scared. Just when things were going nicely
too!'

'Is it all right to leave here just now?' said Mr. Stick,
doubtfully. 'Suppose whoever was here yesterday is still
here – they might pop down into the dungeons when
we're gone.'

'Well, they're not here,' said Mrs. Stick, firmly. 'Use
your common sense, if you've got any – wouldn't our
Edgar yell the place down if he was being kept prisoner

on this little island – and wouldn't we hear him? I tell yo
he must have been taken off in a boat, together with a
the other things that are gone. And I don't like it.'

'All right, all right!' said Mr. Stick, in a grumbli
tone. 'That boy's always a nuisance – always in si
trouble of some sort.'

'How can you talk of poor Edgar like that?' cried M
Stick. 'Do you think the poor child *likes* being capture
Goodness knows what he's going through – feelir
frightened and lonely without me.'

Julian felt disgusted. Here was Mrs. Stick talking li
that about old Spotty-Face – and yet she had a little g
down in the dungeons – a child much younger tha
Edgar! What a beast she was.

'What about Tinker?' said Mr. Stick, in a sulky ton
'Better leave him here, hadn't we, to guard the entran
to the dungeons? Not that there will be anyone here,
what you say is right.'

'Oh, we'll leave Tinker,' said Mrs. Stick, setting o
to the boat. Julian saw them embark, leaving the do
behind. Tinker watched them rowing away, his tail wo
down between his legs. Then he turned and ran back
the courtyard, and lay down dolefully in the sun. He w
very uneasy. His ears were cocked and he kept lookir
this way and that. He didn't like this queer island and i
unexpected noises.

Julian tore back to the cave and dropped down th
rope, startling Edgar very much. 'Come outside the cav
and I'll tell you my plans,' said Julian to the others. F
didn't want Edgar to hear them. They all went outsid
Anne had got breakfast ready whilst Julian had bee

gone, and the kettle was boiling away merrily on the little stove.

'Listen!' said Julian. 'The Sticks have gone off in their boat back to the mainland to see if they can find their precious darling Edgar. Mrs. Stick is all hot and bothered because she thinks someone's gone off with him and she's afraid the poor boy will be feeling frightened and lonely!'

'*Well!*' said George. 'Doesn't she think that the little kidnapped girl must be feeling much worse? What a horrid woman she is!'

'You're right,' said Julian. 'Well, what I propose to do is this – we'll go down into the dungeons now and rescue the little girl – and bring her here to our cave for breakfast. Then we'll take her off in our boat, go to the police, find out where her parents are, and telephone to them that she is safe.'

'What shall we do with Edgar?' said Anne.

'*I* know!' said George at once. 'We'll put Edgar into the dungeon instead of the little girl! Think how astonished the Sticks will be to find the little girl gone – and their dear Edgar shut up in the dungeon instead!'

'Oooh! – that *is* a good idea,' said Anne, and all the others laughed and agreed.

'You stay here, Anne, and cut some more bread and butter for the little girl,' said Julian. He knew that Anne hated going down into the dungeons.

Anne nodded, pleased.

'All right, I will. I'll just take the kettle off for a bit too, or else the water will boil away.'

They all went back into the cave. 'Come with us, Edgar,' said Julian. 'You come too, Timmy.'

'Where you going to take me?' said Edgar suspiciously.

'A nice cosy, comfortable place, where cows can't get at you,' said Julian. 'Come on! Buck up.'

'Gr-r-r-r-r,' said Timmy, his nose against Edgar's leg. Edgar got up in a hurry.

They all went up the rope, one after another, though Edgar was terribly scared, and was sure he couldn't. But with Timmy snapping at his ankles below, he climbed up the rope remarkably quickly, and was hauled out at the top by Julian.

'Now, quick march!' said Julian, who wanted to get

erything over before the Sticks thought of returning.
nd quick march it was, over the cliffs, over the low wall
f the castle, and down into the courtyard.

'I'm not going down into them dungeons with you,'
id Edgar, in alarm.

'You are, Spotty-Face,' said Julian, amiably.

'Where's my Pa and Ma?' said Edgar, looking anxi-
sly all round.

'Those cows have got them, I expect,' said George.
he ones that came and mooed at you and threw things,
u know.'

Everyone giggled, except Edgar, who looked worried
d pale. He did not like this kind of adventure at all.
he children came to the dungeon entrance, and found
at the Sticks had not only closed down the stone that
ened the way to the dungeons, but had also dragged
avy rocks across it.

'Blow your parents!' said Julian, to Edgar. 'Making a
t of trouble for everybody. Come on, stir yourself – all
nds to these stones. Edgar, pull when we pull. Go
! You'll get into trouble if you don't.'

Edgar pulled with the rest, and one by one the rocks
ere moved away. Then the heavy trapdoor stone was
uled up too, and the flight of steps was exposed lead-
g down into darkness.

'There's Tinker!' suddenly cried Edgar, pointing to
bush some distance away. Tinker was there, hiding,
ite terrified at seeing Timothy again.

'Fat lot of good Stinker is,' said Julian. 'No, Timmy –
u're not to eat him. Stay here! He wouldn't taste nice
you did eat him!'

Timothy was sorry not to be able to chase Stink
round and round the island. If he couldn't chase rabbi
he might at least be allowed to chase Stinker!

They all went down into the dungeons. Julian's wh
chalk-marks were still on the rocky walls, so it was ea
to find the way to the cave-like room where the childre
last summer, had found piles of golden ingots. They f
sure that the little kidnapped girl had been put there, f
this cave had a big wooden door that could be bolted
the outside.

They came to the door. It was well and truly bolte
There was no sound from inside. Everyone halted o
side and Timmy scratched at the door, whining gent
He knew there was someone inside.

'Hallo, there!' shouted Julian, in a loud and chee
ful voice. 'Are you all right? We've come to resc
you.'

There was a scrambling noise, as if someone had got
from a stool. Then a small voice sounded from the ca

'Hallo! Who are you? Oh, do please rescue me! I
so lonely and frightened!'

'Just undoing the door!' called back Julian, che
fully. 'We're all children out here, so don't be afra
You'll soon be safe.'

He shot back the bolts, and flung open the door. I
side the cave, which was lighted by a lantern, sto
a small girl, with a scared little white face, and large d;
eyes. Dark red hair tumbled round her cheeks, and s
had evidently been crying bitterly, for her face was di
and tear-stained.

Dick went to her and put his arm round her. 'Eve

thing's all right now,' he said. 'You're safe. We'll take you back to your mother.'

'I do want her, I do, I do,' said the little girl, and tears ran down her cheeks again. 'Why am I here? I don't like being here.'

'Oh, it's just an adventure you've had,' said Julian. 'It's over now – at least, nearly over. There's still a bit of it left – a nice bit, though. We want you to come and have breakfast with us in our cave. We've a lovely cave.'

'Oh, have you?' said the little girl, rubbing her eyes. 'I want to go with you, I like you, but I didn't like those other people.'

'Of course you didn't,' said George. 'Look! This is Timothy, our dog. He wants to be friends with you.'

'What a simply lovely dog!' said the little girl, and flung her arms around Timmy's neck. He licked her in delight. George was pleased. She put her arm round the little girl.

'What's your name?' she said.

'Jennifer Mary Armstrong,' said the little girl. 'What's yours?'

'George,' said George, and the little girl nodded, thinking that George was a boy, not a girl, for she was dressed in shorts just like Julian and Dick, and her hair was short, too, though very curly.

The others told her their names – and then she looked at Edgar, who had said nothing.

'This is Spotty-Face,' said Julian. 'He isn't a friend of ours. It was his father and mother who put you here,

Jennifer. Now we are going to leave him here in your place. It will be such a pleasant surprise for them, won't it?'

Edgar gave a yell of dismay and tried to back away – but Julian gave him a strong shove that sent him flying into the cave.

'There's only one way to teach people like you and your parents that wickedness doesn't pay!' said the boy, grimly. 'And that is to punish you hard. People like you don't understand kindness. You think it's just being soft and silly. All right – you can have a taste of what Jennifer has had. It will do you good, and do your parents a lot of good too! Good-bye!'

Edgar began to howl dismally as Julian bolted the big wooden door top and bottom. 'I shall starve!' he wailed.

'Oh no, you won't,' said Julian. 'There's plenty of food and water in there, so help yourself. It would do you good to go hungry for a while, all the same.'

'Mind the cows don't get you!' called Dick, and he gave a realistic moo that startled Jennifer very much, for the echoes came mooing round too.

'It's all right – only the echoes,' said George, smiling at her in the torch-light. Edgar howled away in the cave, sobbing like a baby.

'Little coward, isn't he?' said Julian. 'Come on – let's get back. I'm awfully hungry for my breakfast.'

'So am I,' said Jennifer, slipping her small hand into Julian's. 'I wasn't hungry at all in that cave – but now I am. Thank you for rescuing me.'

'Don't mention it,' said Julian, grinning at her. 'It's a real pleasure – and an even greater one to put old

Spotty-Face there instead of you. Nice to give the Sticks a dose of their own medicine.'

Jennifer didn't know what he meant, but the others did, and they chuckled. They made their way back through the dark, musty passages of the dungeons, passing many caves, big and small, on the way. They came at last to the flight of steps and went up them into the dazzling sunlight.

'Oh!' said Jennifer, breathing in great gulps of the fresh, sea-smelling air. 'Oh! This is lovely! Where am I?'

'On our island,' said George. 'And this is our ruined castle. You were brought here last night in a boat. We heard you scream, and that's how we guessed you were being made a prisoner.'

They walked to the cliff, and Jennifer was amazed at the way they disappeared down the knotted rope. She was eager to try too, and soon slid down into the cave.

'Nice kid, isn't she?' said Julian to George. 'My word, she's had even more of an adventure than we have!'

Chapter Twenty-One

A VISIT TO THE POLICE STATION

ANNE liked Jennifer very much, and gave her a hug and a kiss. Jennifer looked round the well-furnished cave in amazement and wonder – and then she gave a scream of surprise and joy. She pointed to Anne's neatly-made bed, on which sat a number of beautiful dolls, and a large teddy-bear.

'My dolls!' she said. 'Oh, and Teddy, too! Oh, oh, where did you get them? I've missed them so! Oh Josephine and Angela and Rosebud and Marigold, have you missed me?'

She flung herself on the dolls. Anne was very interested to hear their names. 'I've looked after them well,' she told Jennifer. 'They're quite all right.'

'Oh, thank you,' said the little girl, happily. 'I do think you're all nice. Oh, I say – what a lovely breakfast!'

It was. Anne had opened a tin of salmon, two tins of peaches, a tin of milk, cut some bread and butter, and made a big jug of cocoa. Jennifer sat down and began to eat. She was very hungry, and as she ate, she began to lose her paleness and look rosy and happy.

The children talked busily as they ate. Jennifer told them about herself.

'I was playing in the garden with my nurse,' she said, 'and suddenly, when nurse had gone indoors to fetch something, a man climbed over the wall, threw a shawl round my head, and took me away. We lived by the sea, you know, and I soon heard the sound of the waves splashing on the shore, and I knew I was being put into a boat. I was taken to a big ship, and locked down in a cabin for two days. Then I suppose I was brought here one night. I was so frightened that I screamed.'

'That was the scream we heard,' said George. 'It was lucky we heard it. We had thought there was smuggling going on here, in our island – we didn't guess it was a case of kidnapping, till we heard you scream – though we had found your trunk with your clothes and toys.'

'I don't know how the man got those,' said Jennifer. 'Maybe one of our maids helped him. There was one I didn't like at all. She was called Sarah Stick.'

'Ah!' said Julian, at once. 'That's the one, then! It was Mr. and Mrs. Stick who brought you here. Sarah Stick, your maid, must be some relation of theirs. They must have been in the pay of someone else, I should think – someone who had a ship, and could bring you here to hide you.'

'Jolly good hiding-place, too,' said George. 'No one but us would ever have found it out.'

They ate all their breakfast, made some more cocoa, and discussed their future plans.

'We'll take our boat and go to the mainland this morning,' said Julian. 'We'll go straight to the police station with Jennifer. I expect the newspapers are full of her disappearance, and the police will recognize her at once.'

'I hope they catch the Sticks,' said George. 'I hope they won't disappear into thin air as soon as they hear that Jennifer is found.'

'Yes – we must warn the police of that,' said Julian, thoughtfully. 'Better not spread the news abroad till the Sticks are caught. I wonder where they are.'

'Let's get the boat now,' said Dick. 'There's no point in waiting about. Jennifer's parents will be thrilled to know she is safe.'

'I don't really want to leave this lovely cave,' said Jennifer, who was thoroughly enjoying herself now. 'I wish I lived here, too. Are you going to come back to the island and live here, Julian?'

'Well, we shall come back for a few days more, I expect,' said Julian. 'You see, our aunt's home is empty at the moment because she is away ill and our uncle is with her. So we might as well stay on our island till they come back.'

'Oh, *could* I come back with you?' begged Jennifer, her small round face alight with joy at the thought of living in a cave on an island with these nice children and their lovely dog. 'Oh, do let me! I would so like it. And I do so love Timmy.'

'I don't expect your parents would let you, especially after you've just been kidnapped,' said Julian. 'But you can ask them, if you like.'

They all went to the boat and got in. Julian pushed off. George steered the boat in and out of the rocks. They saw the wreck, which interested Jenny very much indeed. She badly wanted to stop, but the others thought they ought to get to land as quickly as possible.

Soon they were near the beach. Alf, the fisher-boy was there. He saw them and waved. He ran to help them to pull in their boat.

'I was coming out in my boat this morning,' he said. 'Your father's back, Master George. But not your mother. She's getting better, they say, and will be back in a week's time.'

'Well, what's my father come back for?' demanded George, in surprise.

'He got worried because nobody answered the telephone,' explained Alf. 'He came down and asked me where you all were. I didn't tell him, of course. I kept your secret. But I was just coming out to warn you this morning. He got back last night – and wasn't he wild? No one here to give him any food – all the house upside down and half the things gone! He's at the police station now.'

'Golly!' said George. 'That's just where *we* are going too! We shall meet him there. Oh dear, I do hope he won't be in an awful temper. You just can't do anything with my father when he's cross.'

'Come on!' said Julian. 'It's a good thing, in a way, that your father is here, George – we can explain everything to him and to the police at the same time.'

They left Alf, who looked very surprised to see Jennifer with the others. He couldn't make out where she had come from. Certainly she had not started out to the island with them – but she had come back in their boat. How was that? It seemed very mysterious to Alf.

The children arrived at the police station and marched in, much to the surprise of the policeman there.

'Hallo!' he said. 'What's the matter? Been doing a burglary, or something, and come to own up?'

'Listen!' said George, suddenly, hearing a loud voice in the room next to theirs. 'That's Father's voice!'

She darted to the door. The policeman called to her, shocked. 'Now don't you go in there. The Inspector's in here. Come over here special, he has, and mustn't be interrupted.'

But George had flung open the door and gone inside. Her father turned and saw her. He rose to his feet. 'George! Where have you been? How dare you go away like this and leave the house and everything! It's been robbed right and left! I've just been telling the Inspector about all the things that have been stolen.'

'Don't worry, Father,' said George. 'Really don't worry. We've found them all. How's Mother?'

'Better, much better,' said her father, still looking amazed and angry. 'Thank goodness I can go back and tell her where you are. She kept asking me about you all, and I had to keep saying you were all right, so as not to worry her – but I hadn't any idea what was happening to you or where you had gone. I feel very displeased with you. Where were you?'

'On the island,' said George, looking rather sulky, as she often did when her father was angry with her. 'Julian will tell you all about it.'

Julian came in, followed by Dick, Anne, Jennifer and Timothy. The Inspector, a big, clever-looking man with dark eyes under shaggy eyebrows, looked at them all closely. When he saw Jennifer, he stared hard – and then suddenly rose to his feet.

'What's your name, little girl?' he said.

'Jennifer Mary Armstrong,' said Jenny, in a surprised voice.

'Bless us all!' said the Inspector, in a startled voice.

'Here's the child the whole country is looking for – and she walks in here as cool as a cucumber! Lands sakes where did she come from?'

'What do you mean?' said George's father, looking surprised. 'What child is the whole country looking for? I haven't read the papers for some days.'

'Then you don't know about little Jenny Armstrong being kidnapped?' said the Inspector, sitting down and pulling Jenny near him. 'She's the daughter of Harry Armstrong, the millionaire, you know. Well, somebody kidnapped her and wants a hundred thousand pound ransom for her. My word, we've combed the country for her – and here she is, as merry as you please. Well, I'm blessed – this is the queerest thing I ever knew. Where have you been, little Missy?'

'On the island,' said Jenny. 'Julian – you tell it all.'

So Julian told the whole story from beginning to end. The policeman from outside came in, and took notes down as he spoke. Everyone listened in amazement. As for George's father, his eyes nearly fell out of his head. What adventures these children did have, to be sure and how well they managed everything!

'And do you happen to know who was the owner of the ship that brought little Miss Jenny along – the one that sent the boat off to the wreck and put her there for the Sticks to take?' asked the Inspector.

'No,' said Julian. 'All we heard was that the *Roamer* was coming that night.'

'A-ha!' said the Inspector, with great satisfaction in his voice. 'Aha and oho! We know the *Roamer* all right – a ship we've been watching for some time – owned by somebody we're very, very suspicious of – we think he's dabbling in a whole lot of shady deals. Now this is very good news indeed. The thing is – where are the Sticks – and how can we catch them red-handed, now you've got Miss Jenny out of their clutches? They'll probably deny everything.'

'I know how we could catch them,' said Julian, quickly. 'We've left their nasty son, Edgar, locked in the same dungeon where they put Jenny. If only one of us could pass the word to the Sticks, that that is where Edgar is, they'd go back to the island all right, and go right into the dungeons – so if you found them there, it wouldn't be much good them denying that they don't know anything about the island, and have never been there.'

'That would certainly make things a lot easier,' said the Inspector. He pressed a bell and another policeman came into the room. The Inspector gave him a full description of Mr. and Mrs. Stick, and told him to watch the countryside round about, and report when they were found.

'Then, Master Julian, you might like to go and have a little conversation with them about their son, Edgar,' said the Inspector, smiling. 'If they do go back to the island, we shall follow them, and get all the evidence we want. Thank you for your very great help. Now we must telephone to Miss Jenny's parents and tell them she is safe.'

'She can come back to Kirrin Cottage with us,' said George's father, still looking rather dazed at all that had happened. 'I've got Joanna, our old cook, to come back for a while to put things straight, so there will be someone there to see to the children. They must all come back.'

'Well, Father,' said George, firmly, 'we will come back just for today, but we plan to spend another week on Kirrin Island till Mother comes back. She said we could, and we are having such a fine time there. Let Joanna stay at Kirrin Cottage and keep it in order and get it ready for Mother when she comes home – she won't want the bother of looking after us too. We can look after ourselves on the island.'

'I certainly think these children deserve a reward for the good work they have done,' remarked the Inspector, and that settled the matter.

'Very well,' said George's father, 'you can all go off to the island again – but you must be back when your Mother returns, George.'

'Of course I will,' said George. 'I badly want to see Mother. But home isn't nice without her. I would rather be on our island.'

'And I want to be there, too,' said Jenny, unexpectedly. 'Ask my parents to come to Kirrin, please – so that I can ask them if I can go with the other children.'

'I'll do my best,' said the Inspector, grinning at the five children. They liked him very much. George's father stood up.

'Come along!' he said. 'I want my lunch. All this has made me feel hungry. We'll go and see if Joanna has got anything for us.'

Off they all went, talking nineteen to the dozen, making George's poor father feel quite bewildered. He always seemed to get into the middle of some adventure when these children were about!

Chapter Twenty-Two

BACK TO KIRRIN ISLAND!

Soon everyone was at Kirrin Cottage. Joanna, the old cook they had had before, gave them a good welcome, and listened to their adventures in astonishment, getting the lunch ready all the while.

It was whilst they were having lunch that Julian, looking out of the window, suddenly caught sight of a figure he knew very well – someone skulking along behind the hedge.

'Old Pa Stick!' he said, and jumped up. 'I'll go after him. Stay here, everyone.'

He went out of the house, ran round a corner and came face to face with Mr. Stick.

'Do you want to know where Edgar is?' said Julian, mysteriously.

Mr. Stick looked startled. He stared at Julian not knowing what to say.

'He's down in the dungeons, locked in that cave,' said Julian, even more mysteriously.

'You don't know nothin' about Edgar,' said Mr. Stick. 'Where have you been? Didn't you go home?'

'Never you mind,' said Julian. 'But if you want to find Edgar – look in that cave!'

Mr. Stick gave the boy a glare and left him. Julian hurried indoors and rang up the police station. He felt sure that Mr. Stick would tell Mrs. Stick what he had

said, and that Mrs. Stick would insist on going back to
the island to see if what he had said was true. So all that
needed to be done was for the police to keep a watch on
the boats along the shore and see when the Sticks left.

The children finished their dinner, and Uncle Quentin announced that he must return to his wife, who would
want to know his news. 'I'll tell her you are having a fine
time on the island,' he said, 'and we can tell her all the
extraordinary details when she returns home, better.'

He left in a car, and the children wondered whether
they might now return to their island or not. But they
decided to wait a little, for they did not know what to do
with Jennifer.

Very soon a large car drove up and stopped outside the

gate of Kirrin Cottage. Out jumped a tall man with dark red hair, and a pretty woman. 'They must be your father and mother, Jenny,' said Julian.

They were – and Jennifer got so many hugs and kisses that she quite lost her breath. She had to tell her story again and again, and her father could not thank Julian and the others enough for all they had done.

'Ask me for any reward you like!' he said, 'and you can have it. I shall never, never be able to tell you how grateful I am to you for rescuing our little Jenny.'

'Oh – we don't want anything, thank you,' said Julian, politely. 'We enjoyed it all very much. We like adventures.'

'Ah, but you *must* tell me something you want!' said Jenny's father.

Julian glanced round at the others. He knew that none of them wanted a reward. Jenny nudged him hard and nodded her head vigorously. Julian laughed.

'Well,' he said, 'there *is* one thing we'd all like very much.'

'It's granted before you ask it!' said Jenny's father.

'Will you let Jenny come and spend a week with us on our island?' said Julian. Jenny gave a squeal and pressed Julian's arm very hard between her two small hands.

Jenny's parents looked rather taken-aback. 'Well,' said her father, 'well – she's just been kidnapped, you know – and we don't feel inclined to let her out of our sight at the moment – and. . . .'

'You promised Julian you'd grant what he asked, you promised, Daddy,' said Jenny, urgently. 'Oh please do let me. I've always wanted to live on an island. And this

one has got a perfectly marvellous cave, and a wonderful
ruined castle, and the dungeons where I was kept, and –'

'And we take Timothy, our dog, with us,' said Julian.
'See what a big powerful fellow he is – nobody could come
to much harm with Timmy about – could they, Tim?'

'Woof!' said Timothy, in his deepest voice.

'Well, you can go, Jenny, on one condition,' said the
little girl's father at last, 'and that is that I and your
mother come over tomorrow and spend the day on the
island, to see that everything is all right for you.'

'Oh, thank you, thank you, Daddy!' cried Jenny, and
danced round the room in delight. A whole week on the
island with these new friends of hers, and Timmy the
dog! What could be lovelier?

'Jenny can stay here the night, can't she?' said George.
'You'll be staying at the hotel, I suppose?'

Soon Jenny's parents left and went to the police station to get all the details of the kidnapping. The children
went to see if Joanna was going to make cakes for tea.

Just about tea-time there came a knocking at the door.
A large policeman stood outside.

'Is Master Julian here?' he said. 'Oh, you're the boy
we want, sir. The Sticks have just left for the island in
their boat, and we've got ours on the beach to follow. But
we don't think we know the way in and out of those hidden rocks that lie all round Kirrin Island. Could you or
Miss Georgina guide us, do you think?'

'I'm Master George, not Miss Georgina,' said George,
in a cold voice.

'Sorry, sir,' said the policeman, with a grin. 'Well, could
you come too?'

'We'll all come!' said Dick, jumping up. 'I want to go back to the dear old island and sleep in our cave again tonight. Why should we miss a single night? We can send the boat back tomorrow for Jenny's people. We'll all come.'

The policeman was a little doubtful about so many coming in his boat, but the children insisted, and as there was no time to waste, they all ended in crowding into the boat, with three big policemen. Timmy lay down at George's feet as usual.

George guided the boat as cleverly as ever, and soon they landed in the usual little sandy cove. The Sticks had evidently gone round by the wreck as usual, and landed on the rockier part.

'Now, no noise,' said Julian, warningly. They all went quietly towards the ruin, and came into the courtyard. There was no sign of the Sticks.

'We'll go down underground,' said Julian. 'I've got my torch. I expect the Sticks are down there already, letting out dear Edgar.'

They went down the steps into the dark dungeons. Anne went too, this time, holding on to the hand of one of the big policemen. They moved quietly through the long, dark, winding passages.

They came at last to the door of the cave in which they had imprisoned Edgar. It was still bolted at the top and bottom!

'Look!' said Julian, in a whisper, shining his torch on to the door. 'The Sticks haven't been down here yet.'

'Sh!' said George, as Timmy growled softly. 'There's someone coming. Hide! It's the Sticks, I expect.'

They all hid behind the wall that ran near by. They could hear footsteps coming nearer, and then the voice of Mrs. Stick raised in anger.

'If my Edgar's locked in there, I'll have something to say about it! Locking up a poor innocent boy like that! I don't understand it. If he's there, where's the girl? You answer me that. Where's the girl? It's my belief that the boss has done some double-crossing to do us out of our share of the money. Didn't he say that he'd give us a hundred pounds if we kept Jenny Armstrong for a week? Now I think he must have sent someone to this island, played tricks on us, taken the girl himself and locked up our Edgar.'

'You may be right, Clara,' said Mr. Stick, his voice coming nearer and nearer. 'But how did this boy Julian know where Edgar was? There's a lot I don't understand about all this.'

Now the Sticks were right at the door of the cave, with Stinker at their heels. Stinker smelt the others in hiding and whined in fear. Mr. Stick kicked him.

'Stop it! It's enough to hear our own voices echoing away all round without your whines too!'

Mrs. Stick was calling out loudly: 'Edgar! Are you there? Edgar!'

'Ma! Yes, I'm here!' yelled Edgar. 'Let me out, quick! I'm proper scared. Let me out!'

Mrs. Stick undid the bolts at once and flung open the door. By the light of the lantern in the cave she saw Edgar. He ran to her, half-crying.

'Who put you here?' demanded Mrs. Stick. 'You tell your Pa and he'll knock their heads off, won't you, Pa?

Putting a poor frightened child into a dark cave like th
It's a wicked thing to do!'

Suddenly the Stick family had the fright of their lives
for a large policeman stepped out of the shadows, tor
in one hand and notebook in the other!

'Ah!' said the policeman, in a deep voice. 'You'
right, Clara Stick. To shut up a poor frightened chi
in that cave *is* a wicked thing to do – and that's wh:
you did, isn't it? You put Jenny Armstrong there
She's only a little girl. This boy of yours knew he wasn
coming to any harm – but that little girl was scared t
death!'

Mrs. Stick stood there, opening and shutting her mout
like a goldfish, not finding a word to say. Mr. Stic
squealed like a rat caught in a corner.

'We're copped! It's a trap, that's what it is. We'
copped!'

Edgar began to cry, sobbing like a four-year-old. Th
other children felt disgusted with him. The Sticks sud
denly caught sight of all the children when Julian switche
on his torch.

'Snakes alive, there's all the children – and there
Jenny Armstrong too!' said Mr. Stick, in a tone of th
greatest amazement. 'What's all this? What's happen
ing? Who shut up Edgar?'

'We'll tell you the answers when we get to the polic
station,' said the big policeman. 'Now, are you comin
quietly?'

The Sticks went quietly, Edgar sobbing away to him
self. He imagined his mother and father in prison, an
he himself sent to a hard and difficult school, not allowe

to see his mother for years. Not that that would matter, for the Sticks, both mother and father, were no good to Edgar, and had taught him nothing but bad things. There might be a chance for the wretched boy if he were kept away from them, and set a good example instead of a bad one.

'We shan't be coming back with you,' said Julian, politely, to the policemen. 'We're staying here the night. You could go back in the Sticks' boat. They know the way all right. Take their dog with you. There he is – Stinker, we call him.'

The Sticks' boat was found and the policemen, the two grown-up Sticks and Edgar got in. Stinker jumped in too, glad to get away from the glare of Timothy's green eyes.

Julian pushed the boat out. 'Good-bye!' he called, and the other children waved good-bye, too. 'Good-bye, Mr. Stick, don't go kidnapping any more children. Good-bye, Mrs. Stick, look after Edgar better, in case *he* gets kidnapped again! Good-bye, Spotty-Face, try and be a better boy! Good-bye, Stinker, do get a bath as soon as possible. Good-bye!'

The policemen grinned and waved. The Sticks said not a word, nor did they wave. They sat sullen and angry, trying to work out in their minds what had happened to make things end up like this.

The boat rounded a high rock and was soon out of sight. 'Hurrah!' said Dick. 'They've gone – gone for ever! We've got our island to ourselves at last. Come on, Jenny, we'll show you all over it! What a lovely time we're going to have.'

They raced away, happy and carefree, five children and a dog, alone on an island they loved. And we will leave them there to enjoy their week's happiness. They really do deserve it!

A complete list of the FAMOUS FIVE
ADVENTURES by Enid Blyton

1   FIVE ON A TREASURE ISLAND
2   FIVE GO ADVENTURING AGAIN
3   FIVE RUN AWAY TOGETHER
4   FIVE GO TO SMUGGLER'S TOP
5   FIVE GO OFF IN A CARAVAN
6   FIVE ON KIRRIN ISLAND AGAIN
7   FIVE GO OFF TO CAMP
8   FIVE GET INTO TROUBLE
9   FIVE FALL INTO ADVENTURE
10 FIVE ON A HIKE TOGETHER
11 FIVE HAVE A WONDERFUL TIME
12 FIVE GO DOWN TO THE SEA
13 FIVE GO TO MYSTERY MOOR
14 FIVE HAVE PLENTY OF FUN
15 FIVE ON A SECRET TRAIL
16 FIVE GO TO BILLYCOCK HILL
17 FIVE GET INTO A FIX
18 FIVE ON FINNISTON FARM
19 FIVE GO TO DEMON'S ROCKS
20 FIVE HAVE A MYSTERY TO SOLVE
21 FIVE ARE TOGETHER AGAIN

If any of these is not available in a Knight
paperback edition, it can be bought in a
hard-cover edition published by
Brockhampton Press.